**This book is to be returned on or before
the last date stamped below.**

LIBREX

Pete Johnson has been a film extra, a film critic for Radio 1, an English teacher and a journalist. However, his dream was always to be a writer. At the age of ten, he wrote a fan letter to Dodie Smith, author of *The Hundred and One Dalmatians*, and they wrote to each other for many years. Dodie Smith was the first person to encourage him to be a writer.

He has written many books for children, as well as plays for the theatre and Radio 4, and is a popular visitor to schools and libraries.

Books by Pete Johnson

THE COOL BOFFIN
FAKING IT
THE HERO GAME
I'D RATHER BE FAMOUS
MIND READER DOUBLE
THE PROTECTORS
TEN HOURS TO LIVE

For younger readers

PIRATE BROTHER

THE HERO GAME

PETE JOHNSON

PUFFIN

PUFFIN BOOKS

Published by the Penguin Group
Penguin Books Ltd, 80 Strand, London WC2R 0RL, England
Penguin Group (USA) Inc., 375 Hudson Street, New York, New York 10014, USA
Penguin Group (Canada), 10 Alcorn Avenue, Toronto, Ontario, Canada M4V 3B2
(a division of Pearson Penguin Canada Inc.)
Penguin Ireland, 25 St Stephen's Green, Dublin 2, Ireland (a division of Penguin Books Ltd)
Penguin Group (Australia), 250 Camberwell Road, Camberwell, Victoria 3124, Australia
(a division of Pearson Australia Group Pty Ltd)
Penguin Books India Pvt Ltd, 11 Community Centre, Panchsheel Park, New Delhi – 110 017, India
Penguin Group (NZ), cnr Airborne and Rosedale Roads, Albany, Auckland 1310, New Zealand
(a division of Pearson New Zealand Ltd)
Penguin Books (South Africa) (Pty) Ltd, 24 Sturdee Avenue, Rosebank, Johannesburg 2196, South Africa

Penguin Books Ltd, Registered Offices: 80 Strand, London WC2R 0RL, England

www.penguin.com

First published 2005
1

Copyright © Pete Johnson, 2005
All rights reserved

The moral right of the author has been asserted

Set in 11.5/15.5 pt Linotype Goudy
Typeset by Palimpsest Book Production Limited, Polmont, Stirlingshire
Made and printed in England by Clays Ltd, St Ives plc

British Library Cataloguing in Publication Data
A CIP catalogue record for this book is available from the British Library

ISBN 0–141–31817–1

This book is dedicated to my mum – and the memory of my dad, with deep gratitude

Compassion is the basis of all morality
– Artur Schopenhauer

Chapter One

It all started when I became a time traveller.

Yes, for a while I really could burn off into the past whenever I wanted. But don't worry, this isn't going to turn into one of those tales in which I discover a time machine in my back garden one sunny morning.

No, this is a real story. And perhaps because it's real I didn't stay a time traveller for long – and one day I came crashing down to earth all right.

I want to tell you all about that. But first I must admit something: up to the age of eleven there was only one interesting thing about me – my eyes. One of them is green, the other blue. People would come up to me demanding, 'So how come you've got wonky eyes, then?'

Well, how did I know? I even thought of making up something. 'When I was a baby my mum took me to the fair, where this mad wizard put a spell on me . . .'

Apart from my wonky eyes, there was nothing special

about me at all. According to my classmates, anyhow.

Yet they hardly knew me. And that was my fault. I was just so incredibly, ridiculously shy.

Other people in my class didn't seem to have any doubts about themselves at all. I'd marvel at their confidence – and wonder where it had come from. And how could I get some?

I went around with a couple of other boys who, like me, were outcasts. But I didn't have any close mates. No, I lived inside my head. I have to say, it was great there, far more interesting and exciting than school.

Once this PE teacher said to me, 'Charlie, you always look as if you've just woken up or are about to fall asleep.' That was me all right: dreaming my way through every single day.

My mum used to worry about me. She was always nagging me to bring friends home. Until one day Dad said, 'Leave the lad alone. I was a loner at his age too. He'll change in his own good time. Just like I did.'

And Dad was now a salesman, for which you needed masses of self-assurance. So my shyness was just a phase. One day I'd outgrow it. That cheered me up greatly.

Then, when I was eleven and a half, my life changed forever.

I came home from school as usual. But as soon as I saw Mum, I got this horrible, queasy feeling. Something was wrong. And I was right.

Dad had done a runner.

He'd packed up and gone to live with a woman he'd met at work. Mum had no idea he was seeing someone else. And neither had I. It came right out of the blue for both of us.

I felt betrayed and confused and very, very angry. Then, a few days after Dad had left, he sent me a postcard, just as if he were on holiday or something. He said he'd be in touch again soon. And he was. He rang me on my birthday.

Mum answered the phone. I heard her having this very stilted conversation with him. Then she called me. I wanted to talk to Dad so badly, but I also wanted to punish him. I kept thinking of how he'd gone off without a word to me. The hurt inside me hardened. And in the end I didn't say a single word to him – and I never got another chance because, two days later, he died in a car accident.

After that was not a good time at all. I sank into a gloom that never lifted. I could feel it brooding over me all the time. Mum did try and talk to me about what had happened. But the awkwardness between us was just unbearable.

I was so sick of everything – but especially of being me.

Chapter Two

I was at my lowest ebb when – to my surprise – Grandad turned up.

My grandad (Mum's dad) was one of those people you like instantly. I can't say exactly why. Maybe it was because you knew he was someone you could totally trust.

A tall, softly spoken man, he always dressed very smartly and correctly. So, if he wore his blue blazer, there'd always be a white handkerchief sprouting out of his top pocket as well. And he was the politest person I'd ever met. You could never go through a door after him. He'd always tap you on the shoulder and say, 'No, you go first.'

Yet he wasn't at all stuffy. There was usually a twinkle in his eyes. And that reminds me of something we had in common: wonky eyes. He too had one green eye and one blue eye. And on my birthday cards he'd write: 'To another member of the Wonky Eyes Association. Love, Grandad.'

I don't remember his first wife very well at all. I just

know she was ill for a long time. And after she died, Grandad travelled – he was away a long time, actually. I've still got all the amazing postcards that he sent me.

Then he re-married. And he and his wife – who I call Nan – travelled for a bit too. The trips stopped after he had a cancer scare, though. He and Nan moved into this little village in Hertfordshire. I loved staying in their ancient cottage.

He and Nan came to Dad's funeral. After which, I didn't think I'd see Grandad for a while. But, as I told you, he did turn up again – on his own, this time – a couple of weeks later. I thought he'd come to check up on Mum. But, as I found out later, it was me he was especially worried about.

And on Saturday afternoon he took me to London. We were in this restaurant and we'd just finished our starters when Grandad asked me something about my dad . . . and suddenly it was as if I were at the centre of an explosion. Honestly, that's the only way I can describe it. It was as if all the pain and terrible guilt about my dad that I'd been bottling up for weeks just burst out of me.

I started crying so hard I couldn't breathe for a few seconds. Then I remember Grandad standing over me, patting me on the shoulder and saying, 'You're all right, Charlie, you're all right.' I'd never, ever lost control of myself like that before – and in public too.

But afterwards Grandad said that all those feelings had been eating away at my insides – and it was very good to release them at last. He made me feel as if I'd achieved something. He also said, 'Your father wouldn't want you to feel like this, you know. He really wouldn't.'

Later, when I'd recovered myself, Grandad asked me if I wanted to go anywhere, and I said, 'Yes, the Imperial War Museum.' It was somewhere I'd never visited before. And I thought Grandad would be interested, as he was a retired airline pilot. Also, he'd done things in World War II. But he'd never said much about that to me . . . until late that afternoon.

After we'd gone round the Imperial War Museum, we went to a cafe. Then Grandad, puffing away on his little black pipe (which he said he wasn't allowed to smoke at home), started telling me about how he'd been a fighter pilot during World War II – when he was only eighteen.

He didn't show off or anything. For instance, talking about his first time in the air facing the Germans, he said, 'It was pure luck I wasn't shot down – I had no skill at all.'

It was like a window opening into the past.

A few days after he'd gone back, I received a letter from Grandad. He said he'd been so stirred by our chat that he'd got out his old album of photographs from his days as a fighter pilot. There was one photo that had just taken his breath away. He thought it would have a similar effect on me. That's why he'd enclosed it.

It was of three pilots in their smart uniforms, standing in front of a plane. There was a label underneath giving the names: Sammy, Geoff and . . . the third name was Grandad's – Eddie. But it could have been mine.

The resemblance between us was just uncanny . . . same nose, same mouth, same expression – even that kind of half-smile I do.

It was as if I'd somehow met up with myself sixty years ago.

I was here now.

Yet I was also this courageous fighter pilot, saving the country from Nazi tyranny.

It was dead exciting.

And I felt even closer to Grandad.

Well, in a way, I *was* him.

Chapter Three

'Knights of the air.'

That's what Winston Churchill called the fighter pilots – also known as 'fighter boys', because most of them were so young – in 1940.

And one of those 'knights of the air' was my grandad. He was one of the people who prevented us being occupied by the Nazis.

Hitler already had most of Europe under Nazi rule, and he'd drawn up these really detailed plans for the invasion of Britain. Grandad told me that Hitler had even selected the English hotel that was to be his headquarters. Talk about confidence!

All that stood between Hitler and victory was the RAF.

So, in August 1940 Hitler sent massive numbers of German planes to smash the RAF. During the next two months, battles took place over the English Channel and across an eight-hundred-mile front, from Edinburgh to Exeter.

People could look up and see, just above their roofs, the most intense air fighting ever. It must have been a bit like being in a siege.

And Grandad was one of the people who'd shown the world that Hitler could be beaten.

After Dad died, Grandad would travel up from his little village home and 'look in' on Mum and me every single week. And I was eager to hear more about his days as a fighter pilot. So he'd tell me about terrifying dogfights and the time a bullet smashed right through his cockpit and out the other side. And I just lapped all the stories up. Couldn't get enough of them. I'd even ask to hear the same ones again, the way little kids do. And afterwards I'd repeat them to myself and live in them.

In fact, I never wanted to come out of those stories – especially to go to school, which I felt more disconnected from than ever. Although she'd tried throwing herself into her work, Mum was feeling pretty miserable too. So then, one day, Grandad arrived with an amazing idea.

There was a house for sale in his village that he thought would be ideal for us. So why didn't we move there?

His invitation burst into my life like a wonderful rocket. I was completely enthusiastic about it from the beginning. Mum needed a little more time. There was her job at the solicitor's for instance . . . but Grandad helped set up a new job for her at a solicitor's near him. And soon Mum could see the value of giving up our tired, used lives here and making a completely fresh start.

She told me she was reverting back to her old surname – which, of course, was also Grandad's. Immediately I decided I'd have that surname too. And we settled into our new world so quickly. Mum threw herself into village life right away. And I decided I'd try and make a much better impression at my new school in the nearby town: an all-boys secondary school. (Both Mum and I would have preferred a mixed school, but there wasn't one close by.)

Grandad saw me off that first morning and said, 'Going solo into a new school isn't easy – it takes some courage. But you'll do it, all right.'

And somehow I did. Still, I was greatly helped by the first lesson being history. Would you believe it: they were studying World War II! All my shyness just melted away. I had masses to say. Afterwards I casually mentioned to the teacher that Grandad had been a fighter pilot. She asked if he would come and give the class a talk about his experiences.

At first Grandad turned me down flat; he said he hadn't spoken about that time to anyone but me for years and years. But eventually he agreed to go. My classmates were pretty sceptical too. I think they were expecting some wizened old geezer who'd be dead boring.

In fact, Grandad was a really down-to-earth speaker. He began by stating, 'I was the very worst student you could ever meet – much worse than anyone here. Left school at fourteen with no education at all . . . Not surprising that I felt a bit inferior, bit second-rate.'

I could totally relate to this feeling – so, I think, could quite a few others in my class.

'I didn't have the right posh background to join the Air Force. But then I heard about the Volunteer Reserve Scheme. They paid you to learn to fly. Well, after about eighty hours of that I went to Whitehall and said to the Air Ministry that I wanted to be a fighter pilot. Now the government may have been desperate for fighter pilots – but not that desperate. I went in front of this panel, who looked at me very doubtfully because I was so poorly educated. I would have to sit a special exam. Now, I'd never passed an exam in my life, but this time I just had to succeed . . .'

Grandad went on and on in this way. And although he got a bit lyrical when he was talking about his beloved Spitfires (he even claimed they had a soul), he had everyone gripped, especially when he told some of his exciting stories.

Afterwards came the questions. One boy asked, 'So what was it like killing people, then?'

Grandad didn't baulk at this question at all. He just said quietly, 'I shot at aircraft, I didn't shoot at people . . . didn't think of a person in it. Once, though, I did shoot down a chap over the sea. I saw where he'd gone down and I flew up alongside him, but it wasn't in me to go on shooting at him.'

Another said, with a cheeky grin, 'So what's it like being a big hero, then?'

He replied, 'There were thousands of heroes, but I wasn't one of them. The heroes were all those who didn't come back. I was one of the very lucky ones. I was just doing a job, that's all.' Then he added, 'We all knew we had to win and that we'd just fight on and on until we did.'

Later, Grandad passed round some of his snapshots: they were a bit smudged and were all in black and white. But seeing such bravery up close sent a shiver down the spine all right.

It was so long ago now that those times had the glow of a legend about them, and Grandad himself seemed as mythical as one of the knights of the Round Table.

At the end, this boy said to him, 'Please may I shake your hand?' Soon everyone wanted to shake Grandad's hand. Then people asked him for his autograph. I stood beside him, grinning like an idiot, I was so proud. And a little of his magic settled on me. Somehow I was a part of those days too.

Afterwards Grandad just muttered, 'Well, I think we just about got away with that one.'

In fact, he was such a hit he was soon asked back to my school. The local paper ran a two-page feature on him. He was interviewed four times (in one year) on the local radio, then he was featured on a Channel 4 programme about fighter pilots. He was even invited to open a fête, but every request that came in was first referred to me. 'Got to check with my agent,' he said.

That was what he called me: his 'agent'.

Of course, basking in the glow of Grandad's celebrity, I had no trouble finding mates at school. And girls even started showing an interest in me. They'd smile at me in town and . . . well, that was it, really. But it was good, anyhow.

Now I was someone worth knowing.

Only I wasn't. Not really. You could say that my own life wasn't any good so I had borrowed Grandad's instead. But he'd had such a big life that it really didn't matter.

And he did claim that I'd helped *him* too. He once told me, 'If it hadn't been for you, I'd just be sitting in a deckchair with a straw hat on, listening to my bones creaking. Thank you, Charlie.' Yes, he actually thanked me.

He also claimed that I helped him recall things. I was certainly always pestering him for some extra details about those days. And it was as if there were all this extra stuff tucked right at the back of his head that had to be coaxed out.

I wanted to know everything about his war.

Grandad gave me some of his precious pictures from wartime – including one of him in his sheepskin flying jacket that is my absolute favourite – and I stuck them all on my wall. I'd look at them before I fell asleep, and then I'd have dreams . . . well, you won't believe the number of missions I've flown.

Embarrassing confession time! I kept a pad by my bed. And as soon as I woke up I'd write down every detail of my dream as a fighter pilot before it slipped out of my memory. Don't laugh.

Anyway, two years slipped past. The two happiest of my life, without any question.

Then came Grandad's eightieth birthday. I planned such a special surprise for him.

Chapter Four

Grandad's eightieth birthday. It was half past nine on a Saturday morning. The grass was all hazed with frost. It was freezing. And I was loitering near his cottage . . . the end one of three.

Grandad's front garden won a prize last year. Most of the year round it's thick with flowers. And even on a dull February day, when everywhere else is dreary and colourless, there's a great sweep of golden daffodils to greet you. Somehow, the flowers always come out especially early in this garden.

Suddenly the front door opened and out rushed Grandad, smartly dressed as ever, with Gertie, his West Highland terrier, jumping about excitedly beside him. Nan had said she'd try and get him to leave especially early today.

I stayed hidden until he was out of sight. Then Nan signalled to me to come over. She was loving all this undercover stuff. We quickly went over the details of Grandad's surprise, after which she left as well.

Most houses lack character – in my opinion, anyway. But Grandad's cottage was full of interesting things.

So, in his hallway there's this mask he picked up on his travels in Africa and a collection of fishing rods. Then in the sitting room there are massive posters of *Casablanca* and *Brief Encounter* (his two favourite films) and more large photographs of places he's visited.

Tons of family snaps too, of course, and a magnificent painting of a Spitfire. But, oddly enough, just one photograph from Grandad's RAF days, and that's a group picture, with him slightly out of focus. I guess Grandad thought that plastering his wartime exploits all over the walls was too much like showing off. (He keeps all his medals upstairs in a drawer too.)

Still, every single wall had something interesting on it. And if I ever bought a house, I'd decorate it in what I call Grandad's style. I'd try and have the same atmosphere too: with the kettle always boiling and the fire crackling away so cheerfully . . . There's something in this house that just makes you want to stay longer.

I waited inside Grandad's house until a car pulled up – right on time. A white-haired man got out and for a moment I thought that was him. But he opened the car door and another, even older man sort of shuffled out. He stood looking at the house for a moment, an album tucked under his arm, and muttered something to the driver, who got back in the car. Then the old man walked slowly forward.

15

He was shorter than Grandad but bulkier, his face more weather-beaten, while only a few wisps of grey hair flowed back from his forehead. He was dressed exactly like Grandad, though, in a smart blazer and tie.

When I opened the door he tottered back, his eyes popping out of his head. For one awful moment I thought he was going to keel over. But he recovered himself.

'You should have warned me, Charlie,' he croaked. 'You're the spitting image of him . . . you've even got the same eyes . . . It's just uncanny . . . For a moment there, I thought I'd stepped into the twilight zone.' He gave a wheezy chuckle. Then he said, 'So he's got no idea I'm turning up here today?'

'None at all,' I said.

'Well, I hope the shock's not too much for him,' he said. 'You do realize we haven't set eyes on each other for nearly sixty years. Bit of luck you finding my message on the Internet, wasn't it?'

It was just by the sheerest chance that I'd come across his request for members of his squadron in World War II to get in contact. And when I saw his name – Geoff Hays – my stomach did a flip. Could that be the same person Grandad was always talking about and who featured with him in so many of the photographs?

I got in touch on Grandad's behalf – he won't have anything to do with the Internet, says he's got better things to do in his declining years – and discovered this was indeed the Geoff Hays who'd been Grandad's best mate all those years ago. 'Life was so uncertain in those days,' he said. 'You didn't know where you were going next and you just lost touch with people. I can't wait to see your grandad.' Then we hatched this plan.

I took Geoff into the kitchen and made him a cup of tea; he was just telling me how he'd gone on to the Internet to expand his horizons when I heard a key in the lock. I sprang up, mouthed at Geoff to stay silent and rushed into the hallway.

Grandad didn't look very astonished at me popping up; I was always dropping in – I even had my own key. 'Oh, hello there,' said Grandad. 'Is Nan looking after you?'

'Nan had to go out,' I said. I didn't need to say any more. Nan was always off somewhere. Mum said just watching Nan made her tired. 'I wanted to wish you a very happy birthday . . .'

Grandad waved a dismissive hand. 'I've had too many birthdays.'

'And I've got a surprise for you in the kitchen . . . Don't worry, it's not a cake. We weren't allowed to have one with all your candles on. It's against the fire regulations.'

'Very funny,' said Grandad, bending down and unhooking Gertie's lead. 'What's this surprise, then?'

At this point Gertie shot past us and pushed open the kitchen door. She let out a volley of surprised barks. Grandad gave me a puzzled look. 'Better see who's in there, Grandad,' I said.

He half marched into the kitchen. Geoff stood up and said in his low voice, 'Smiler Marriott, I presume. I do hope you remember me.'

Grandad stared at him, then made this funny little

sound, like someone laughing and gasping at the same time. 'Well, I'm blowed,' he cried in a shocked, cracked voice. 'Geoff Hays . . . I don't believe it.'

'The years have been kind to you,' said Geoff. 'You've still got all your own hair – not like me.'

'Oh, this is one of my wigs,' said Grandad.

'Is it?' For a moment Geoff believed him, then he saw Grandad's face. 'You haven't changed . . . still larking about.'

He stepped forward and tapped Grandad on the shoulder.

'Remember my first mission?' he asked in a hoarse whisper. 'I was shaking with nerves. I'd seen some chaps who were burnt. I was a mess until you took me in hand. You always batted for the underdog. You said to me, "If only one plane comes back today, it's going to be yours."' He swallowed hard. His neck started to wobble. 'Do you remember that?' he quavered.

Grandad put an arm round him. 'Not going to start weeping on my shoulder, are you?' he said teasingly. Geoff gave a shaky laugh at that. And they staggered into the sitting room like two old mates who'd had a bit too much to drink.

The photo albums didn't come out until after Nan had got back and we'd eaten Grandad's birthday lunch. Then they both really pored over those photographs. They began reciting the names of all the other 'chaps' in the pictures. They could still name practically everyone. It was incredible. I don't think I could still remember the names of everyone I was at infant school with – and that wasn't even ten years ago.

But all the stories were shot through with sadness as they recalled all their mates who had died. Some never even reached the age of twenty.

'If there were six of you having breakfast together before going into action,' said Geoff, 'you knew that one of you probably wouldn't be there for supper.'

'I wouldn't have liked those odds,' I said.

'You just didn't allow yourself to brood on it,' said Grandad.

'And Smiler here kept our spirits up,' said Geoff.

'I never knew that was your nickname,' I said to Grandad.

'Well, I've got to keep a few secrets,' he replied.

Geoff enjoyed himself so much, he rang up his son to ask if he could stay a while longer. I thought that was such a weird role-reversal. When Geoff's son finally came to collect him, Geoff and Grandad didn't hug each other or anything, they just punched each other on the shoulder and Geoff whispered, 'We shan't lose touch again.'

Afterwards Grandad sat there, shaking his head in wonderment. 'And you managed to find Geoff through the Internet.' He said 'the Internet' the way you might say 'black magic'.

'You'd really like the Internet if you gave it a chance. I can teach you about it if you like.'

'Maybe tomorrow,' said Grandad. 'Today, just let me sit here and savour the best birthday present I've ever had.'

So that was a bit of a result! We chatted away for ages

about things Geoff had talked about. Then I remembered one particular thing Geoff had said: 'After we've gone, who'll know all this stuff?' And suddenly I thought: these stories are too good to just vanish away – I wanted them to live on. So why didn't I write down Grandad's tales – only not as a conventional book. No, I'd make it a graphic novel. Loads of people at my school read them. So that would give it a much wider readership.

Move over, Tintin – here come the true adventures of Smiler Marriott.

When I told Grandad about my plan, he laughed for about five minutes. But he thought it was a good idea, all the same. There was just one problem: I couldn't draw to save my life. So I'd need a collaborator.

One name immediately sprang into my head: Yolande.

Actually, I have to admit, her name was in my head pretty often these days.

You see, Yolande . . . but she deserves a chapter all to herself.

Chapter Five

Me – and Yolande.

Until last month I'd never have thought I had a chance with her. I'd spotted her around the village. She was sixteen (two years older than me) and absolutely gorgeous. So, of course, way out of my league.

But then my school joined up with the local girls' school to put on a production of *An Inspector Calls* by J. B. Priestley. Well, I auditioned for the role of the inspector. Got to the last three, but in the end I lost the part to – Yolande.

She rushed up to me afterwards and said, 'Just wanted to say I thought you were brilliant, but if they have a girl playing the part, they'll get in the newspapers . . . and a black girl too.' She smiled. 'Well, think how much more publicity they'll get for that.' (Yolande was right: the production even got a write-up in *Stage*.)

I did get offered another part, as a kind of consolation

prize, and she and I had lots of little chats during rehearsals. In fact, we were often together. I'd say there was definitely a spark between us. There certainly was on my part, anyhow. In fact, I couldn't take my eyes off her. She's got this heart-shaped face and huge green eyes . . . and when she talks to you there's a real warmth in her voice that sets your heart racing.

Anyway, one day this boy from my school called Callum turned up. He was in Year Eleven, but he wasn't in the play. He just sat watching it. When I asked someone what he was doing there, they whispered back that he was Yolande's boyfriend.

I noticed this greedy look in his eyes every time he stared at her, as if he couldn't get enough of her. The thing was, I felt exactly the same way.

Then, on the last night of the play, I discovered that Yolande and Callum had broken up. He'd dumped her, apparently. I was really shocked and felt very sorry for Yolande. I was a bit happy as well, though, for with Callum off the scene . . .

Yolande and I had exchanged addresses and mobile numbers . . . but I thought I'd wait awhile until I saw her again . . . and asked her out. In other words, I dithered.

But now, at last, I had an excuse to call round, as Yolande was a really talented artist. (In fact, she'd won prizes.) So I could ask her about the graphic novel – then just slip in, 'Oh, by the way, how would you like to go out with me one night?'

Grandad smiled a little bit when I mentioned Yolande's

name. I hadn't discussed her much, even with him. But he'd sort of guessed how I felt.

'Yes, you go and see Yolande . . . that's an excellent idea,' he said. Then he added with a little twinkle, 'And the very best of luck.'

As I rang the doorbell I felt a strange tightness in my stomach. This was far more nerve-racking than acting on stage. Still, it was the very first time I'd ever asked a girl out.

She opened the door. 'Charlie!' Her voice rose in surprise.

'Just thought I'd call round, see how you are . . . Haven't seen you for ages.'

'No, well, I've had flu, so I haven't been out much.'

'How are you now?'

'Oh, much better. Look, come in, Charlie.'

We went into the sitting room. Her parents were out. I was pleased about that. I was nervous enough without having to make conversation with them as well. She made me a cup of coffee and I told her about Grandad's reunion with Geoff. She listened intently. 'And did your Grandad recognize him right away?'

'Practically. He just looked at him for a couple of seconds and then . . . well, he couldn't believe his eyes.'

'Charlie the magician.' Yolande said this with a teasing smile – but in quite an affectionate way too.

Then I asked her about collaborating with me on the graphic novel. She seemed flattered that I'd thought of her.

'Of course I'll give you half the profits,' I said.

'Going to make my fortune, am I?'

'You'll be a millionaire before you're twenty,' I said wildly.

'That sounds good to me.'

She smiled. And I decided this was the right moment to ask her out. 'I was just wondering if you'd like to go out with me sometime?'

Yolande's smile quickly faded. But she wasn't saying anything either. So I rattled on.

'Maybe we could go out for a meal one night . . . or to the cinema, or wherever you like, really. You just name it, I'll go there. I don't care.' I gave a desperate laugh, while I observed a red flush creeping up Yolande's neck.

'I wasn't expecting this at all,' she said in a tight, little voice.

'Weren't you?' I looked away.

'It's a huge compliment . . . but the thing is, I'm really not interested in going out with anyone right now.'

Inside my head I let out a great howl of disappointment. But I just murmured, 'So you're turning me down, then?' I tried saying this as a kind of joke.

'No, I'm turning all boys down,' she quickly replied.

Was she just saying that to make me feel better? I really didn't know. Maybe she was still nursing a broken heart over Callum. Was she hoping he'd come back to her one day?

'I'd really like to work on the graphic novel with you, though. Am I still hired?'

'Oh yes, I'm going to get some of my interviews with Grandad on tape first, but then I'll be in touch again.'

She beamed at me like a lighthouse. 'Can't wait to get started . . . thanks so much for thinking of me.'

Then, just as I was leaving, I said lightly, 'If ever you decide to return to the wonderful world of dating . . .'

She smiled faintly. 'You'll be the first to know.'

Chapter Six

The following night Grandad rang me. 'How about a spot of interviewing tonight? Does that fit in with your plans?' He always made it sound as if I had about eight offers for my company every night. 'Bring your tape recorder round and we'll really get down to it,' he went on.

When I arrived, Nan was sitting in the lounge too. 'I see he's about to talk your head off again,' she said.

'You'd better show me some respect,' cried Grandad, 'as I'm about to become a cartoon character. Now, will Yolande be doing the artwork?'

'Yes, she will.'

'Who's Yolande?' demanded Nan.

'The girl we saw in Charlie's school play . . . Played the inspector.'

'I asked her out yesterday,' I announced suddenly.

'Did you?' cried Grandad. 'Any luck?'

'Not especially,' I said. 'She turned me down flat. She

did say it was nothing personal. She was taking a break from all boys.'

'Very sensible,' murmured Nan.

'I think she might still be getting over her last boyfriend,' I said.

'Well, that shows she's a girl of deep feelings . . . Now don't lose hope, Charlie,' said Grandad. 'Faint heart never won fair lady and all that. Your nan said "No" when I first asked her to marry me, you know. But I kept on asking her.'

'And in the end he wore me down,' said Nan. 'Of course, I've been regretting it ever since.' She and Grandad were always bantering with each other, yet I'd caught them holding hands more than once.

'So you mustn't give up,' said Grandad.

I grinned. 'I won't.'

Then he added, so casually it just took my breath away, 'Got to go to hospital for a few days to be prodded about and generally have my time wasted.'

'But why?' I gasped.

Grandad stood up and muttered, half to himself, 'Oh, some silly, time-wasting nonsense.'

'They think his cancer might have come back,' said Nan quietly.

I was too numb with shock to say anything at first. So I just sat there in this zombie-like daze. It was the very last thing I'd expected. I knew Grandad had had a cancer scare, but that was years ago. And he was so sprightly – everyone said so. He couldn't be seriously ill. Not Grandad. He was unstoppable.

'How long will you be in there for?' I asked.

'Not sure exactly,' said Grandad. 'Hoping they'll give me time off for good behaviour.' He smiled.

But I didn't smile back. Instead, this terrible heaviness came over me. I couldn't begin to imagine my life without Grandad. He was absolutely vital to me.

'Now don't look like that,' said Grandad. 'Doctors exaggerate, you know. They're always trying to put the wind up you.'

'How do you feel now, Grandad?' I asked. 'Tell me exactly.'

'I think I'll last the night,' he replied in his laconic way.

'I'll come and see you every day,' I said.

'Now I'd much rather you didn't,' Grandad replied firmly. 'It'd only depress you – and me. No, much better to wait until I'm back.'

'They won't keep him in long,' cut in Nan.

'What I'd like,' went on Grandad, 'is for you to have started this cartoon book with the charming Yolande, and have something to show me when I come back. That would be the best medicine for me.' Then, before I could reply, Grandad declared, 'So it's all settled, isn't it? And I think we've spoken about it quite long enough now.'

'Seems to me,' said Nan, 'that you're the one doing all the talking.' Then she got up and tousled my hair. 'I'll leave you boys to get on with it.' She often called us both 'boys' and acted as if I were Grandad's mate, come round to call for him. I suppose I *was* his mate really, and his grandson, and his agent and, now, his biographer.

Nan left. I put on the tape recorder and Grandad went and stood in front of the fireplace. He stared into it for a few moments, as if he were summoning up the past. Then he turned round, hands in pockets, head jutting slightly forward. 'Right, fire away with your first question, Charlie.'

I could tell how impatient he was for us to take off to the other world that we shared. And, before long, he and I disappeared inside those stories, and everything else just shrank away. Of course I'd heard them before, but Grandad was adding so much extra detail now, they felt completely fresh to me.

I read this quote once. It said, 'The past is a foreign country.' Not with Grandad it isn't. He makes the past seem really close, as if it's just round the corner. Not far away or strange at all.

'Inside us,' said Grandad, 'there's no past or present . . . it all belongs together.'

When he finally stopped, it was like being jolted back to reality. I hated that. I think he did too.

At the front door Nan hissed, 'I'll let you know how he's doing – but he really would rather you didn't come and see him in the hospital. You know what he's like.'

Yes, I knew.

He didn't want Mum seeing him either. In fact, he was adamant about that too. 'I feel awful not visiting him,' said Mum, 'but what can I do? I don't want to upset him.'

Grandad's absence left a massive hole in both our lives. At least Mum had her amateur dramatics to throw herself into. She was directing a play for the very first time.

And I had my graphic novel.

A couple of days after I'd been to see Yolande, she rang. She wanted to do some preliminary sketches of Smiler, and would I act as her model? So I sat round Yolande's house, while she drew all these cartoon pictures of me. That was kind of weird – but good fun too.

And we chatted about everything – except me asking her out. I even told her about Grandad going into hospital. 'And he doesn't want any visitors,' I said.

'Very wise,' said Yolande. 'Being ill is a private thing. I wouldn't want anyone to come and see me either.'

'I'll remember that,' I said.

'Make sure you do,' she grinned.

Then I showed Yolande the little sampler I'd written for our graphic novel. I thought you might like to see it too. So here it is:

SMILER IN ACTION

by

Charlie Marriott and Yolande Turner

'Scramble, scramble!' shouts a voice. That's the signal that means battle in the skies against Hitler's Luftwaffe.

'Looks like Hitler wants to play,' says eighteen-year-old Smiler. It's his first mission and he's very scared. Not that anyone could ever guess that.

Smiler races to his Spitfire. His parachute is hanging on the wing top. He puts it on. The ground crew start up the engine. He runs his hand along the wing of the Spitfire.

'Hello there, how are we tonight?' He always speaks

to his Spitfire as if she's a beautiful woman. His mates do too. Vibrations start humming all through the Spitfire as if she's coming alive. The door is closed. He sits strapped in his cramped, tiny cockpit.

He is one of a squadron of twelve Spitfires. Smiler eases the throttle open. It is take-off. 'You're a wonderful girl,' he murmurs to the Spitfire. He talks to her all the time.

The first time he flew a Spitfire, he'd been terrified, though. She went off like a rocket and he couldn't get the airspeed down again. Took him a few times to get used to her. But now, he thought, she was a magical plane.

The airport is left far behind now as twelve Spitfires climb away on full power. Then control is calling. The controller's voice is calm. But his news is terrifying. 'OVER A HUNDRED ENEMY PLANES ARE APPROACHING.'

And then Smiler sees them in the far distance: a great plague of German bombers. They're really putting on a show tonight. 'Twelve against a hundred. Not the greatest odds,' murmurs Smiler. Yet he knows they have to win.

So there is nothing for it but to get stuck in. He remembers he must never fly straight for longer than fifteen seconds. If he does, he'll almost certainly be shot down. He's got to hurl his plane across the sky.

A voice on his earphones says, 'OK, boys, in we go.'

A new power surges through him. He's flying into deadly combat. He's flying for his life . . .

And that's as far as I got. I don't know what you thought of it. But anyway, I didn't carry on with it.

In fact, I never wrote another word.

Chapter Seven

It was Yolande's idea.

On the local radio there's this lunchtime show, where people go on and ask for help in finding old friends. And she suggested I talk on Grandad's behalf.

I liked the idea at once. After my last success at finding Geoff I was eager to track down more old comrades, and what a tonic for Grandad it would be when he came home.

So I rang up the radio station and they invited me on, over half-term. The host was Richie Allen. On air, if he was any more syrupy he could be spread on toast. Off air, he's the coldest person I've ever met, with these dead eyes.

But he asked all the questions I'd prepared on the phone with his researcher and my mouth didn't freeze up as I'd feared. He ended by inviting anyone who'd served with Grandad to ring up the radio station.

Next day I was put in touch with three callers. The first one, Russell Wilkins, had been a fighter pilot with

Grandad. He spoke in glowing terms about Smiler's unfailing good humour. I couldn't help feeling a bit proud when he said that. Russell had a very bad back at the moment – his voice sounded quite frail too – but he hoped when he was better to pop over and see Grandad. (He lived in Ipswich.)

The next caller was a woman. Her father had died last year, but he'd often spoken of his days as a pilot and the great comradeship of those times. One of the names he'd mentioned was Grandad's.

And, finally, there was a man who introduced himself as Mr Perkins.

'I was so eager to get in touch,' he said in this smooth, fruity voice, 'even though I didn't serve with your grandfather during the war or any of that. But I was at school with him, way back in the 1930s, for two years. A long, long time ago, but I've never forgotten him or those years at Highsmith.'

This was a real find. Grandad hardly ever spoke about his schooldays except to say what a lousy pupil he'd been. I supposed that he had too many sad memories, especially with his mother dying when he was eleven. It would be great to interview someone who knew him then and to fill in some of the blanks.

Another piece of luck (or so I thought at the time) was that Mr Perkins lived only about seven miles away, in Shenleigh. 'I moved here after my wife died. My son and his family aren't far away. And I'm settling into a quiet life here.'

When I asked if I could interview him, he suggested

Friday. He sounded nearly as eager as me. 'There's a bus that stops at the end of my road and it calls at your village. Takes forever, though, I'm afraid.'

'That doesn't matter,' I said, 'as I'll probably cycle anyhow.'

I decided I wouldn't tell Nan or Mum about this meeting. I'd just surprise them all with a few funny stories about Grandad's schooldays. I was sure Mr Perkins had some.

I wrote down his phone number proudly in my note-book. And if this were just a tale I'd made up, I'd add that, at the very moment I recorded his number, a shiver of alarm ran up and down my spine as I sensed danger.

But I'm telling you exactly what happened. And I whistled when I wrote Mr Perkins's name in my notebook.

I didn't have a clue what was about to happen.

Not a clue.

Chapter Eight

Mr Perkins lived at the end of a road of prosperous-looking houses, his three-storey home looming majestically over them all. It also had a name: 'The Haven'. I couldn't imagine ever calling my house that. Too pretentious, for a start.

I rang on the doorbell. It played a little tune – 'Rule Britannia' would you believe? That made me smile. I sensed this Mr Perkins was something of an eccentric.

A curtain twitched, then I heard a safety chain being pulled back. A smallish, stooped man leaning on a stick opened the door. He was bald, with a purple-red face, a sharp nose and very staring eyes.

A red handkerchief was tied in a knot under the collar of his ironed, blue shirt and he wore smart black trousers. He stood very still, observing me, then said in a voice like thick cream, 'You can only be Eddie Marriott's grandson.' He stretched out a gloved hand and announced: 'We're in the dining room.'

He led me into a dark room that was crowded with huge furniture including a sideboard with pillars on either side and an enormous oak table. Even the chairs seemed to loom threateningly over us. They had red plush seats and didn't look as if anyone had ever sat on them – or would ever want to either.

'I'm sure a cup of tea will be most welcome after all your cycling,' he said. 'I shan't be long.'

I gazed around. On the mantelpiece was an enormous clock ticking away furiously. Above it was a black-and-white drawing of Mr Perkins in his much younger days. I wondered if he'd drawn that himself. I got up and squinted at the signature.

'That was by my late wife.' Mr Perkins spoke so suddenly, he made me jump. 'She had such a talent for art.' He came lumbering towards me with a tray of tea. I made as if to help him but he said firmly, 'No, I can manage, thank you very much.'

After enquiring whether I took milk and sugar (I do), he slowly poured out my tea and then shakily handed me the cup. He saw me noticing his white, gloved hands. 'I have to wear gloves because of a skin complaint.'

'Oh, I see,' I replied, not sure what else to say.

'It's a non-specific allergy,' he went on, as if I required more information. 'By the way, my name is Maurice, one of those names that it's quite hard to abbreviate.' A brief flash of white teeth. 'Of course, I acquired other nick-names during my schooldays.'

I bet you did, I thought. I'd warmed to Geoff at once. But, for all Maurice Perkins's creaking, antique courtesy,

37

there was something about him I didn't like. Maybe it was the way I felt his eyes on me all the time, as if he were studying me. I suspected I wasn't going to get any hilarious anecdotes from him about Grandad either. This was going to be very dry and very dull.

I wondered too how friendly he and Grandad had been. I just couldn't imagine them being the best of mates.

He took a slow sip of his tea and said, 'Do you know, I read about your grandfather in the local paper just a few weeks ago?'

'Oh, he's always in there,' I replied breezily.

'Is he?' he purred. 'He certainly had an exciting war. I too did my bit, of course. I was in the tanks, but nothing as glamorous as your grandfather, and I was invalided out, unfortunately.' Did his voice have a touch of bitterness in it? I was sure it did. 'Is the tea to your liking?'

'Yeah, it's great,' I lied. It tasted like coloured water.

'I'm always accused of making my tea too weak. My daughter says . . .' But whatever his daughter said was drowned out by the clock screaming that it was three o'clock.

He put on a pair of black-rimmed glasses and peered at me again. 'Time really is twisting about this afternoon . . . It could almost be Eddie Marriott himself sitting opposite me again. How is Eddie?'

I told him briefly about Grandad's illness.

'What a terrible thing old age is – our only consolation is that it's better than the alternative.' He gave a little chuckle then lolled back in his chair. 'Now, what did you wish to ask me?'

'Would you mind if I use a tape recorder?' I put it on the table.

He squinted at it. 'It's so small I shall probably forget it's there . . . so proceed.'

I switched on the tape recorder. 'Could you tell me the first time you met my grandad?'

'I'll never forget it,' he replied. 'Eddie was pushing this boy's face down the school toilet at the time.'

That took the breath out of me all right. What was Perkins talking about? Grandad would never have done that; it just wasn't in his character.

Perkins went smoothly on. 'Oh, I have no doubt the boy deserved it. And Eddie was just dispensing some of his rough justice. But I was scared out of my wits.' He gave a dry laugh. 'Here I was in the middle of term and at a new school. I'd already been warned: "Don't get on the wrong side of Eddie Marriott." I quickly saw why. Anyway, after Eddie had finished ducking this unfortunate chap, he looked up and snapped, "Who the hell are you?" I replied very nervously, "I'm Maurice, but I can see you're busy so I'll come back later." Fortunately this made him laugh.'

Mr Perkins chuckled again, quite oblivious to the way I was shifting about uncomfortably. This image of Grandad as some kind of mad bully wasn't one I recognized at all. Grandad had a strong personality, certainly, but he never threw his weight about. And he liked helping people. Hadn't Geoff said how Grandad always looked out for the underdog?

'Your grandfather wasn't someone to get on the wrong side of . . . I expect he still isn't.'

I could feel my hackles rising now. Just who did this Maurice Perkins think he was, making pronouncements about Grandad?

'Even the teachers were scared of him, you know. But he and I never fell out. The secret with Eddie was always to let him have the last word. I'm sure he still likes having the last word now, doesn't he?' He gave his knowing little smile. I can't tell you how annoying that was.

Why did he keep trying to connect this thuggish, bad-tempered bully he was conjuring up with Grandad today? They weren't alike in any way. Grandad was genial and gentlemanly and funny . . . and I couldn't imagine him ever resembling the creature Mr Perkins was describing.

I began to seriously wonder if there were two Eddie Marriotts. That was very possible – though probably not two who looked exactly like me.

'In the end Eddie was thrown out of school for being unteachable.' That gave me another jolt. 'Yes, he had a crazy streak, but I wouldn't have said he was unteachable, except when he got into one of his tearing rages, of course.'

Mr Perkins's voice fell away. He sat back, patting his stomach as if he'd just finished an especially tasty meal. He'd enjoyed telling me all that stuff about Grandad. In fact, he'd absolutely loved it.

But it wasn't the truth. I was certain of that. No, Mr Perkins had twisted and distorted what had really happened. So now it was as if I were gazing at Grandad through one of those fairground mirrors that made him look all weird and misshapen.

Why was Mr Perkins doing this? Was he jealous of

Grandad? Or did he just want to make himself seem more important than he really was? Perhaps he really had mixed up Grandad with someone else? It was an incredibly long time ago!

Or maybe he was just a mad old coot.

Whatever the reason, all his lies and exaggerations were like a swelling pressure inside my head. And if I stayed any longer, I knew I'd just explode. I switched off the tape recorder.

Mr Perkins looked surprised. 'Don't you have any more questions for me?'

'No, I don't,' I said shortly. 'Thanks for your time.'

'I do hope I haven't upset you at all,' said Mr Perkins. 'I was merely trying to give an honest account of those far-off days.'

But behind his concern I knew he was secretly pleased that I was looking so battered.

'The teachers all regarded your grandfather as a bad egg . . .'

My throat tightened. I couldn't listen to any more of this bile. I shot up, banging into the enormous sideboard in my haste to get out of there.

'One moment please, young man.' Mr Perkins raised a hand as if he were hailing a taxi. 'As I was rather well-spoken, I was bullied unmercifully by some of the other boys. Your grandfather looked out for me.' Suddenly and quite unexpectedly, his voice began to shake with emotion. 'And I am in his debt in another way too. It was he who first introduced me to the Blackshirts . . . but I expect you know all about that.'

I didn't. Who or what were the Blackshirts? Was it some kind of organization? Then I dimly remembered seeing a picture of the Blackshirts once. It showed all these young men marching through the streets of London in a weird uniform. And there was something very disturbing about them. But I couldn't remember exactly what.

I certainly wasn't going to stay another second with this oily poseur. So I just said, 'Got to go now.'

Mr Perkins called something after me that I didn't catch. Didn't want to either. I burst out of that house, sending a great cloud of starlings shrieking up into the air.

I wanted to start shrieking too at the way Mr Perkins had tried to degrade Grandad with his weird stories. All right, Mr Perkins was probably sick in the head, but still he shouldn't be allowed to get away with it.

I tore off on my bike at great speed, the wind making a raging noise in my ears as if sharing in my fury. It was only when I was almost home that I realized I'd left my little tape recorder behind.

But nothing on earth would persuade me to go back for it.

Chapter Nine

Just out of interest, I looked up the Blackshirts on the Internet. In fact, I was directed to a site about the rise of the fascists in the 1930s. That was a shock.

Fascist.

I knew the word, sort of. It's anyone who's very controlling and power-crazed. Like our maths teacher, Mr Martin, who hates you even breathing without his permission. Everyone calls him a 'right fascist' – among many other things.

And I knew there were real-life fascist leaders. Hitler, of course, and Mussolini in Italy too. He was the one who started it all. He said he was the only man who could stop Italy sliding into total chaos. Gave himself a title – *Il Duce* ('The Leader') – and set up the first one-party, totalitarian state.

What I didn't know was that he inspired someone called Oswald Mosley to try and do the same in Britain.

Mosley had been first a Conservative and later a Labour MP. Then he founded a brand-new party in 1932 called the 'British Union of Fascists'.

He looked at all the poverty and unemployment that was sweeping Britain at that time and he declared democracy could never solve those problems. Britain should copy Italy and have a dictator. The person he chose for this task was, er – himself.

He sounded just like a villain from a James Bond film. Especially when he started recruiting his own private army or 'defence force'. They wore very distinctive clothes: black shirts with high, round collars like fencing jackets. This led to them being nicknamed the 'Blackshirts'.

They would march through the streets, yelling patriotic songs and slogans. They would also stick up labels saying really nasty, stupid things against groups like the Jews. Oswald Mosley had decided that the Jews were an internal enemy, and he and his Blackshirt army would 'cleanse' Britain of them.

Blackshirt marches were also deliberately routed through the traditionally Jewish East End of London. Bricks, bottles and stones were thrown by them and at them. At one especially notorious march in Cable Street, over a hundred people were injured. After that the Blackshirts arrived at marches in armour-plated vans, armed with rubber truncheons.

Mosley and his army started acting as if they were running the country. They claimed they were carrying out the will of the people, but in fact they wanted to take away all the freedoms Britain enjoyed. They didn't want the people to have any rights or power. They sounded like total madmen. But they were also highly organized, armed and very dangerous.

How dare Mr Perkins say that Grandad was a part of that! The very idea was laughable. It wasn't worth reading any further, really. But I did – and I discovered that while Oswald Mosley was organizing his Blackshirt army another fascist leader was making headlines: Hitler.

In 1923 Hitler had been thrown into prison for his political activities and he was viewed as a deluded nobody. Eleven years later, he and his party seized total control of Germany – even though less than ten per cent of the German people were actually members of the Nazi Party.

Could Oswald Mosley and his band of supporters ever have done the same in Britain? I'd like to have said 'absolutely not' right away, but one site showed pictures of this massive rally Mosley held at the Albert Hall in London. There were all these Blackshirts marching down the centre aisle, waving Union Jacks and fascist banners. And then this forest of raised arms when Mosley appeared. Apparently they even yelled out, 'Heil Mosley, Heil Mosley.'

Another really sinister picture showed Oswald Mosley inspecting his army of Blackshirts. There he stood in his SS uniform, jackboots gleaming, while all the Blackshirts were heiling him like crazy.

And all that had happened here in Britain.

In the end, the Blackshirts stirred up so much violence that Parliament had to ban the wearing of the Blackshirt uniform and any more fascist meetings. But for a while there were Blackshirt centres and offices around the country. And no one's sure exactly how many members the Blackshirts recruited – although some estimate it as being as many as fifty thousand.

But Grandad would have seen through such a movement right away and been horrified by its racism.

Grandad a Blackshirt? NEVER.

I'd have staked my life on that.

Chapter Ten

Next day Grandad came out of hospital. He was still quite frail, so Nan suggested we visit in shifts, Mum in the afternoon, me in the evening.

I'd been round every day to see Nan and take Gertie for a walk. But that night everything immediately felt different. The whole house just hummed with his presence, even though he didn't come to the door as usual.

Instead, he was in the sitting room in his bright red dressing gown, Gertie flopped across his feet. His head was lowered, so obviously he was having a little nap. I whispered, 'Grandad.' Gertie thumped her tail in welcome. But he didn't stir. I bent over. 'Grandad.'

This time he woke up instantly, peered at me for a moment, then said softly, 'Ah, here he is. Now all my trials and tribulations just vanish away.'

'Charlie can only stay for a few minutes,' announced Nan in the doorway.

'Says who?' demanded Grandad.

'Says me,' she replied.

'Oh, we'll just ignore you, then,' said Grandad.

She laughed and sat down beside me. I could see why she was worried about Grandad. He'd always been thin, but quite suddenly he looked frighteningly thin. And his skin was a strange waxy colour too. He looked like someone who had been very sick indeed.

'How are you feeling?' I asked.

'Terrible,' he replied, so quickly he made me smile. Then he noticed I had something under my arm. 'What's that?'

'It's just the sampler I did . . .'

Immediately there was a big, happy grin on his face. 'Good lad, let's have a look, then.' For the next few minutes he was totally lost in what I'd written. When he put it down he gave me Churchill's victory sign.

'It's very good, isn't it?' said Nan, who'd read it earlier.

Grandad nodded. 'There are just a few tiny little errors and I've also got a couple of suggestions . . .'

Soon we were both wrapped inside his stories once again as I scribbled down all his suggestions. 'This is going to improve it so much,' I said.

'Well, you can't beat an eye-witness account,' said Grandad.

As he said that, I thought suddenly of Mr Perkins. He'd been in my head all day actually. I knew he'd been spouting me a load of rubbish and, as I told you, I didn't believe it for an instant, especially all that stuff about the Blackshirts.

48

But I wanted it exorcized from my mind once and for all. And Grandad was the person to do it. I built up to it carefully, though. First I told him about my spot on the local radio, and then how I'd been contacted by someone else from his squadron and that I had news of another person too.

Grandad could recall both of them instantly. He started describing them and even telling us about things they'd done. 'I remember them both as if I'd seen them only last week,' said Grandad. 'Of course I remember them as they were . . .'

'There was a third person who rang up,' I said. I could hear my breath getting faster. 'He said he was at school with you for two years when you lived at Highsmith.'

'Now we're really going back,' said Nan.

'We certainly are,' cried Grandad. 'What's his name?'

I hesitated. Maybe this was the name of his deadliest enemy and it would make Grandad erupt with fury. And he just wasn't strong enough for that.

'Have you forgotten what he was called?' asked Grandad.

'No, no, it's . . .' and then I said, 'Maurice Perkins,' really quickly as if that would make the name less powerful somehow.

Grandad's face went completely still. 'Maurice Perkins,' And I could tell he was thinking really hard. 'Maurice Perkins.' Grandad repeated the name, only this time very slowly, just as if he were about to cast a spell with it. He closed his eyes for a moment. When he opened them he shook his head. 'I can't see anyone of that name.' He sounded as if he were conducting a seance. 'And I'm absolutely certain I'd have remembered someone called Maurice.'

'Do you think he's a fake, then?'

'I think he may well be, yes,' said Grandad. 'I don't want to sound like I've got a swollen head. But I have got a pretty good memory –'

'You've got a brilliant one,' I interrupted. 'So if you don't remember him, he obviously wasn't there.' My whole body was tingling with relief as I said this.

'He might have read about you in the local papers . . .' suggested Nan.

That's exactly what he must have done. He was obviously some sort of nut job. But a fairly harmless one – if he hadn't tried to tarnish Grandad's reputation with a load of lies. People do that, of course, if you're in the public eye, which Grandad certainly was. They make up things about you to try and pull you down.

I'd read about it once. It's called the 'tall poppy syndrome' – you want to drag down anyone you think is doing better than you. I bet Mr Perkins had a very un-distinguished war record; then he hears me talking about this fighter pilot and he thinks, I'll cause some mischief there. All that stuff about Grandad sticking people's heads down the loo . . . and the Blackshirts.

Of course I had never really believed any of it – not deep down I hadn't. But I felt disloyal to Grandad for even listening to all that garbage.

'Did this man ask you to visit him?' asked Grandad suddenly.

'Well, yes, he did. He said he didn't live very far away.'

Immediately both Grandad and Nan looked worried.

'I think this particular gentleman is really best avoided,' said Grandad slowly.

I didn't tell him that I'd already seen Mr Perkins, because then I'd have had to relate all the things Perkins had said, and they really didn't bear repeating. They were best forgotten.

'He could just be a bit of a crank,' mused Grandad. 'Maybe one day I'll go and see him . . .' A gleam came into his eyes. 'I'll say, "Sir, we are strangers to each other. So why are you pretending otherwise?"'

He was making it into a kind of joke now. But when I got home, Mum knew about Mr Perkins already. Grandad must have called her the second I'd left. So he was obviously more concerned about this than he was letting on.

'It's wonderful, all this work you've done tracking down Grandad's old comrades,' she said. 'But be careful as well – not everyone is what they seem.' She went on to say it would be best if I just avoided Mr Perkins – and to let her know if he tried to get in touch again.

Well, he'd tried already. There was a message on my mobile from the radio station, stating that Mr Perkins had been in touch because I'd left my tape recorder at his house. He was keeping it safe for me and I should give him a ring when I wished to pick it up. They ended the message with Mr Perkins's phone number, although I had that already.

He was obviously keen for me to return.

I thought back to our last meeting. I'd just sat there like a mouse hypnotized by a massive snake, while he hissed all those fake reminiscences. And I hadn't said one word in Grandad's defence.

That felt so shabby now, as if I'd let Grandad down very badly.

How about if I slipped back for my tape recorder but I also let Mr Perkins know I hadn't been fooled by his lies? I needn't stay very long. I'd go in secret too, as Mum would only try and stop me if I told her.

But I'd stop Perkins vandalizing Grandad's good name once and for all.

Chapter Eleven

I rang Mr Perkins. I said I'd collect my tape recorder after school and that I'd probably reach his house at about five o'clock. Meanwhile I told Mum I was going to Yolande's house to work on the graphic novel.

In fact, I did drop in on Yolande after school. She was still in her school uniform. But even imprisoned in that, she looked . . . well, more than beautiful.

She looked pleased to see me too. I even wondered if she might go on to utter those seven magical words, 'Charlie, I will go out with you.' But she didn't. Instead she cried, 'I thought I'd been sacked and you'd got yourself another artist.'

'Actually, I showed Grandad your artwork only last night and he was very impressed. I won't tell you what he said, as it would only turn your head . . . but I've come to ask you . . .'

'Yes.'

'For an alibi.'

Intrigued now, she invited me into her kitchen where I told her about my quest to defeat Mr Perkins. I don't wish to sound melodramatic, but I wanted one person to know where I'd gone. After all, he was a bit of a loony and, well . . . just in case.

She hadn't heard of the Blackshirts, but when I explained about them she was outraged by Mr Perkins's allegations. 'The very idea of your grandad being in that. I went to hear your grandfather talk once . . .'

'I never knew that.'

'It was at the village hall. And he was so sincere and down to earth . . . a real gentleman. So you give Perkins lots of welly from me too tonight . . . Don't actually hit him, though.'

'As if . . .'

'Knock him out with some well-chosen insults. And if the tea he gives you should have a bitter taste . . .'

I laughed. 'Or maybe he'll have bullets concealed in his walking stick. So if I'm not back tonight . . .'

'I'll lead the search party,' said Yolande. 'Afterwards will you come round and tell me what happened?'

'Of course I will.'

Outside it was spitting with rain and it was grey and dark. But I cycled on at a good speed.

And I arrived at his house only a few minutes after five o'clock. He was standing in the doorway, waiting for me this time. He was baring his teeth at me too. You won't be smiling for long, I thought.

He said, 'The dark nights seem to come on so quickly now. Or maybe that's just a sign of old age.'

Chuckling to himself as if he'd made a joke, he led me again into the dining room with the menacing furniture and the noisiest clock I'd ever heard. He waved a gloved hand.

'Here is your tape recorder, all waiting for you . . . and I have the tea ready too.'

I put my tape recorder away. I could feel all this energy coiling up inside me. Was this how Grandad felt when he was about to take off in his Spitfire to face the enemy? Did he just itch to get started? Not that I was comparing facing a German bomber with confronting Mr Perkins. Not in any way.

He returned with the tea tray. Time to fire the first shot. 'All that stuff you said about my grandad . . . the funny thing is, no one else I spoke to remembers him like that at all.'

'I expect they knew him later. I was the only one who was at school with him, wasn't I?' His voice was as silky as ever.

'Yes,' I admitted.

Mr Perkins went on. 'I do hope I didn't give offence, as that wasn't my intention at all.'

Oh yes, I really do believe that one, I thought.

'You claim that my grandad was the one who got you to join the Blackshirts?'

'That's right.' Just the mention of the Blackshirts seemed to perk him up. 'Eddie was already a member, and he was busy recruiting new members, one of which was me.'

'And how long do you claim my grandfather was a Blackshirt?'

'I'm not sure.' He considered. 'Eddie was certainly one for as long as I lived at Highsmith, which was nearly two years.'

Grandad – a Blackshirt for two years. He was really having a laugh now, wasn't he? Grandad wouldn't have been in a fascist organization like that for two hours. It just wasn't in his character.

It was time to put this old coot firmly in his place. 'The odd thing is,' I said, my voice shaking only slightly, 'Grandad doesn't remember you at all.'

I paused to let that sink in. Spots of red suddenly flamed on Mr Perkins's cheeks. But he didn't say a word.

'And Grandad has got the most brilliant memory. I can just say someone's name from sixty years ago, and right away Grandad's telling me all about them – but not you. He's certain he's never heard of you and that you are, in fact –' I paused for emphasis – 'a total and complete impostor.'

Do you know, I could almost feel sorry for Mr Perkins then, because his face nearly fell off with shock. He looked absolutely devastated.

Well, I had no wish to prolong his misery. He'd been found out and that was that, my work here was done.

I got to my feet. 'You really can't go around making up things about people and tarnishing their good name. This must stop right now. All right?'

I expected him to show a little remorse at least. Instead, he folded both hands on his cane and hunched forward. 'I have proof of what I say,' he hissed.

That gave me a start. 'What proof?'

Mr Perkins struggled to his feet. 'I will show you. Follow me.' Then he started tottering off. Where was he going? I followed him to the door. Then I watched him go up the stairs. But I didn't go after him. I just stood at the foot.

What proof could he produce? He couldn't, as he'd made it all up. This was just a ruse. He was furious that I'd found him out, so now he was going to lure me into this room, where he'd be waiting behind the door to strike me on the back of the neck. Or maybe I'd smell a heavy, sweet smell as a chloroform rag was pressed tightly over my mouth and I'd fight and kick but it would be no good . . .

Now I was just being daft. But I had this very strong feeling of danger, all the same.

I couldn't see Mr Perkins now, but I could hear him and his stick shuffling further up the stairs. He called down to me, 'Charlie, do you want to see my proof or not?'

There was a definite note of challenge in his voice now, as if he were saying, 'Are you brave enough to come upstairs?' He was actually daring me.

If Grandad could fly on dangerous missions, surely I was able to walk up one flight of stairs.

All the same, as I followed Mr Perkins I could sense a trap closing round me.

Chapter Twelve

The stairs creaked and groaned. It was almost as if they were talking to me, begging me to go back. He was waiting at the top for me. There were more steps, leading up to the attic. Was that where we were going? Instead, he opened the door nearest to him.

The heavy brown curtains were drawn and it was so dark and dingy, it was hard to make out anything at first. The smell of the room met you at once, though. A stale, bitter stench hung in the air.

Mr Perkins flopped down on to a large swivel chair beside a desk. He reached across the desk and switched on a small green lamp. Also on the desk were a large globe, some pens, pencils, a glass ashtray and two dog chews. The chews seemed a welcome touch of normality in such a spooky room.

'I didn't know you had a dog,' I said.

'I don't. Well, not any more,' said Mr Perkins. 'He died last month.'

And I wouldn't have been altogether surprised if he told me his remains were buried here, it smelt so rancid.

'I still miss him,' murmured Mr Perkins, then he added, 'It's here I allow myself to indulge in my secret vice.'

I jumped. What was he about to tell me now?

'The dreaded weed,' he said. 'A foul habit that I confine to this room . . . Please, do sit down.' I sat down on what was undoubtedly the hardest chair ever made. He put on another pair of glasses, tiny gold ones this time. 'As I get older, the glasses get smaller.' His face twitched. 'Now I have something to show you,' he announced.

It was waiting for me in this room. Something horrible. But what?

'I know exactly where it is,' said Mr Perkins, suddenly authoritative and in command. He pulled out the middle drawer in his desk. Then he reached in and drew out a photo album. 'So many memories here,' he said. He stroked it lovingly in his gloved hands. I wouldn't have been very surprised if he'd started humming a lullaby to it. Instead, bathed in a little pool of green light, he scoured through its pages. His eyes were all screwed up and he was obviously concentrating intently.

I couldn't bear to watch him. I gazed around the room. Books lined one wall and overflowed on to the floor, while stuck to the door and the other walls were old newspaper articles that all seemed to be about asylum seekers.

He muttered something inaudibly. Had he found it? I

wasn't sure. He was making me wait, making it worse. A tense silence seemed to have settled over everything. All I could hear was the faraway sound of a car alarm; it was like a banshee wailing a warning.

A little smile twisted the corners of his mouth. 'Eureka,' he murmured. I watched him remove a photograph from the album. 'I think this will be of great interest to you.' Then he swivelled his chair round to me. There was a little table just in front of the chair. He dropped the photo down on it with a smile of pride, like a dog presenting you with a particularly smelly bone that he had just dug up.

With a huge effort I picked it up. Even before I looked at it, I knew it was going to be something bad. But it was far worse than I'd expected.

Far, far worse.

It showed a group of Blackshirts, their arms all raised in a Nazi salute. And right in the centre of the picture . . . there was no mistaking him.

Grandad's mouth was open as if he were yelling something, while his face was contorted into a look of such rage. He reminded me of those pictures you see sometimes of football hooligans, screaming abuse and throwing bottles . . . Well, that's exactly how Grandad looked – like an evil yob.

I just sat there, staring at it. If I gazed at it long enough, would this all make some kind of sense? Its horror seemed to draw me to it so I couldn't look away. Finally, I cast the picture down. Mr Perkins was watching me with a mixture of anticipation and pleasure. If you've ever seen a cat toying with a half-dead mouse, you'll have a pretty good idea of what the atmosphere was like.

I sat right back in my chair, wanting to be as far away from him and his filthy photo as I could, my arms tightly crossed over my chest. And I kept swallowing because the bitter, musty smell of this room had somehow seeped into my mouth. Now I could actually taste it, and it was making me feel quite sick.

'Did you recognize your grandfather all right?' He couldn't disguise his note of triumph.

I dredged up a voice. 'Yeah, I think that might possibly be him.' I was struggling to make light of it. But my right hand was shaking, slowly, treacherously.

'And did you chance to notice me standing right beside him?' He leant forward, his chair sliding with him.

'I saw you all right,' I said. Even then, he'd looked so sly and self-satisfied. I added ferociously. 'That picture brings back lots of happy memories, does it?'

But he was quite oblivious to my sarcasm. 'Oh yes, it certainly does,' he cried. 'And I don't blame your grandfather for pretending that those times didn't exist.' He sighed heavily. 'There's been so much negative propaganda. I just wish people could know the truth, Charlie. We had our own newspaper, you know. And we had a holiday camp in Sussex. Do you know, for some boys it was the first time they'd ever been to the seaside. And girls came along too. We gave them equality of opportunity, which no else did . . .'

He was trying to make the Blackshirts sound like the Boy Scouts or something. But it wasn't like that at all.

'What about all the hatred the Blackshirts tried to stir up and all the violence they caused?'

'I see you've been doing some research. Good,' said Mr Perkins approvingly. 'And what you've got to remember is, Britain was in a terrible state in the 1930s. People had no jobs, no decent housing, no future . . .'

'And you were going to change all that,' I said mockingly.

'Well, Parliament certainly couldn't do anything. Not with that apology for a prime minister, Ramsay MacDonald, or his successor, Baldwin.' He spat out the name. 'Britain's rebirth could only come about by sweeping aside convention and having a good fascist government.'

'Didn't Hitler put you off fascism just a tiny bit?' I asked.

'Hitler made some very bad mistakes,' he conceded. 'But fascism would have worked out quite differently in England.'

'Only you never got the chance,' I said tauntingly.

'More's the pity,' cried Mr Perkins. 'For half a century I've watched Britain's heritage being eroded away. I've seen the sexual licence of the sixties, the collapse of the family, and now we've got all these immigrants flooding in. Our culture's vanishing in front of our very eyes while all these alien nationalities take over. Well, the British people have had enough.' He pointed at the newspaper-covered walls. 'Just look at all the unrest around us.'

For the first time I peered closely at the cuttings there. A new asylum centre was being set up at a disused office, about two miles away from here. There'd been objections in the local papers about this and there'd also been some sort of protest march. Every picture and article on the subject had been lovingly cut out and displayed by Mr Perkins.

'We cannot allow these people to destroy our country, our way of life,' he cried, his eyes now sharp with hatred. 'Well, I think my son will do something about it.'

'Your son,' I echoed.

'Yes, an absolutely super chap who has followed me into accountancy, but his great passion has always been politics. And he's standing in the by-election here next month . . .'

'As a fascist?'

'As an Independent, actually,' said Mr Perkins. 'Someone who will stand up for local people's rights to refuse this asylum centre. In fact, we're holding a special meeting for some of our key supporters here next Wednesday. So if your grandfather is well enough to join us, he'd be most welcome.'

I gaped at him. Why did he think my grandad would be interested in this?

'I know how difficult life can be for you if you're not wearing the right liberal opinion, and the politically correct police are everywhere. My family and I have withstood a barrage of abuse over the years but . . . we're stronger now. And the tide is turning our way.' A fanatical gleam came into his eyes. 'I am glad I have lived long enough to see these days. But I do understand why so many of our supporters have to remain secret in their allegiance. You can assure your grandfather of my discretion at all times.' His tone was now reassuring and understanding. And he was looking at me with such an awful eagerness, my stomach twisted in horror.

'But my grandad would never want to come to something like that!' I shouted out.

I glanced down at the photograph of Grandad again. He looked so totally unlike himself. And yet it was him. And it was me too in a way. Suddenly I felt a sense of shame so strong I wanted to be sick. No! No! No! This couldn't be true. And I shouldn't even be suspecting Grandad of something like this.

There had to be a logical explanation for that picture. Maybe it was from an open-air play they were putting on. No, unlikely. All right, but there were other reasons. Only I couldn't think in this room that stifled me with its lack of air and fevered opinions and where everything – but especially Grandad – seemed so unreal.

No wonder my head was reeling with so many confused thoughts. And if I didn't get out of there soon I'd SNAP. So there and then, and without a word to Mr Perkins, I bolted out of that room and down the stairs. I fumbled with the door handle. I felt as if I'd been locked up for days.

Outside, the night seemed unnaturally bright. I took a few gulps of air, then cycled away as if my life depended on it. And I just couldn't slow down. It was as if my bike was suddenly enchanted and could only go at one speed: flat out.

It was dark too – that heavy darkness that seems about to fall right on top of you – and normally I'd be more cautious at this time.

But not tonight.

I zoomed along, my legs pounding the pedals as hard as they could. Yet I didn't feel exhilarated or excited by my speed. All I could think about was that I had to get far, far away from what I'd just seen.

I HAD TO GET AWAY.

My whole body felt shaken up, as if I'd just been in a crash.

And then I really was in an accident. I suppose it was inevitable. But, oddly enough, it didn't occur when I was weaving through all these cars and they all kept hooting at me. No, it occurred when I was pedalling like mad down a quiet side road.

No one was about. Then this boy just appeared out of nowhere. He was talking away into a mobile phone as well, completely absorbed in his conversation. And I was heading straight for him. I swerved violently. The next thing I knew, I was thrown forward into the air and right over the handlebars.

Chapter Thirteen

I landed on the road with an almighty splat, my bike clanging down beside me.

The boy I'd almost run into rushed forward. 'Are you all right?'

'Yeah, I'm OK,' I croaked.

I struggled to get up. Leaning on the boy, I staggered across to the pavement. Then the boy darted off to pick up my bike.

I'd attracted a small audience. A group was loitering outside the fish and chip shop, gawping at me. The boy talked into his mobile. 'Ring you back,' he said briefly, then he asked me, 'You sure you're all right?' He sounded really concerned. He was a tall, ginger-haired boy with anxious grey eyes, about my age but serious-looking.

'I just feel a bit shaky, that's all,' I replied.

'You were cycling very fast,' he said.

'I was going like a madman,' I agreed.

'Not that I was looking where I was going either,' he admitted. 'It was just unfortunate that I was taking a really important call at that moment, and it needed my urgent attention.' He made it sound as if he were in MI5 or something, only he didn't say it in a boastful way. He added quietly, tactfully, 'By the way, you've got a piece of gravel behind your ear.'

'Oh, right, thanks.' I started brushing myself down. I was absolutely covered in gravel and my hands were all grazed and black too. The people opposite were still watching me as if I were a professional stunt rider and they were waiting for my next trick. But then, my accident was probably the most exciting thing that had happened here for at least a hundred years.

'Do you want to come back to my home to clean up or pass out?' he asked.

I started to smile. But I don't think he was meaning to be funny. In fact, I'm sure he wasn't. There was something very earnest about him.

'No. I'll be off now, thanks all the same. I'm Charlie, by the way.'

'My name is Raymond.'

We shook hands, as if we'd just been competing in a game of tennis or something.

'Well, best of luck for the rest of your journey,' he said. 'Have you got far to go?'

'Only another couple of miles.'

I got back on the bike, wobbling precariously at first.

Raymond was watching me very concernedly. But then I gave him a quick wave and set off again, though at a greatly reduced speed.

When I got home I felt absolutely shattered. I was glad Mum was out at a rehearsal. I certainly didn't want to talk to her – or to anyone else – about what had happened tonight.

I just wanted to hide myself away for a bit.

I had a shower – or, rather, I started to have one – when my mobile rang. I scrambled to answer it, water dripping everywhere. 'Hello,' I said.

'Oh, you're back, then.' It was Yolande and she sounded distinctly peeved. Of course, I'd promised to see her on my way home. How could I have forgotten that?

'Sorry I didn't drop in but I had an accident on the way home.'

Her tone changed instantly. 'Oh no, what happened?'

I told her all about it. In fact, I made it seem more exciting than it really was. I turned it into a kind of adventure. She was gripped. I enjoyed myself too.

Then she asked about Mr Perkins. I felt myself clamming up immediately. I didn't even want to tell Yolande what I'd seen. This could well make her look at Grandad in a very different way. And at me too, probably.

'Would you rather not talk about it?' She was trying to be understanding, but she sounded hurt as well.

So in the end I said, 'Perkins managed to dredge up this picture of Grandad and him. They were at a rally doing the fascist salute.'

I paused.

'But are you absolutely sure it was your grandad?'

'Oh yes, he looked the spitting image of me. Could have been my twin brother, in fact . . .'

Yolande didn't say anything in reply to that.

'Are you still there?' I whispered.

'Of course I am,' she cried. 'I was just thinking about it . . .'

'I know. I still haven't got my head round it, and I saw it over two hours ago now.'

'It must have been a horrible shock,' she said softly.

'It was. Especially with Perkins leaning over me and gloating about it all. Then he started giving me a party political broadcast for the fascist party.'

'He wasn't trying to convert you?' she asked.

'Oh yeah. And his son's standing as an MP. Not as a member of any political party – but as the MP against the new asylum centre . . .'

'You're joking.'

'No, I'm not. He's talking at a meeting for special supporters at Mr Perkins's house next week. And he only wondered if Grandad wanted to go along. It was so shaming. And all the time he was talking to me, he had this evil smile on his face – I tell you, if snakes could smile, they'd do it exactly like him.'

Yolande didn't say much more and she rang off a few seconds later. I thought I shouldn't have told her. She was obviously really, really disgusted by my revelation. And I couldn't blame her for that.

But about twenty minutes later she rang back. 'You're an army cadet, aren't you?' she demanded.

'I was, for about a year –'

'Now tell me why you joined!' she interrupted. 'No, don't bother, *I*'ll tell *you* why. It's because you liked marching about in a uniform and using guns. You must have had guns.'

'No, but we were allowed to fire air pistols.'

'There you are. All boys like prancing about, pretending to be he-men – weird species that you are. Well, your grandad's no different. He joined the Blackshirts, played at being a soldier as boys do, then discovered its more sinister side and left.'

'But he was doing the Nazi salute.'

'Yes, but he didn't realize that then. He was just having fun saluting people. All Mr Perkins's little snap proves is that your grandad was a Blackshirt for a brief while.' She emphasized those last two words.

'But if you'd seen the way he looked . . .'

'What do you bet he was told to look like that. They said, "Put on a keen expression for the camera."'

'If you say so,' I murmured.

'It's only one little picture, Charlie, but I can see I haven't convinced you.' She rang off before I could reply.

Just before Mum got back, Yolande called for a third time. 'Guess who was a fan of fascist Italy in its early days?' she cried. 'Only Winston Churchill. He admired the way Mussolini cleared the slums and tried to get rid of TB. So if the great Winston Churchill was taken in by fascism for a while, don't be too hard on your grandad.'

'Did you find that out on the Internet?'

'I certainly did. And did you know, some of the English

newspapers supported the Blackshirts at first. There was a headline in one of them that said: "Hurrah for the Blackshirts" . . .'

She talked on while I thought, she's found all that out for me.

FOR ME.

Going to all that trouble proved that she must like me a bit, didn't it? If only she could leave the wretched Callum behind.

Just before she rang off, Yolande said, 'I bet Mr Perkins is gloating now over what he did tonight. And if you believe him, Charlie, he's won.'

'I know. And he's nothing but a malignant weasel, while my grandad's a true hero . . .'

'And a gentleman,' said Yolande. 'There aren't many of them left, but he's one. And if in his youth he joined the Blackshirts, it was because he liked the uniform and marching about. But he never, ever realized what lay behind it.'

That was very likely, wasn't it? And I wanted to believe that so badly.

I just wish, when I'd asked Grandad if he knew Maurice Perkins, that he hadn't looked me straight in the eye and lied his head off.

Chapter Fourteen

Next day after school there was a message from Grandad on my mobile. 'Charlie, can you come round? There's something I need to talk to you about urgently. Don't bother to ring me back, just come over as soon as you can. Thanks very much.'

He sounded extremely serious. Was it about the Blackshirts? That was my first thought. Grandad regretted lying to me and now he was going to tell me the truth. I sprinted over to his house.

'Good of you to get over here so fast. I appreciate it,' said Grandad. Apart from Gertie, he was on his own. We went into the sitting room where the fire was cheering up a grey, chilly afternoon.

'Right out of the blue, I had a call this afternoon from –'

Mr Perkins. In my head I finished the sentence for him. So Grandad knew I'd gone to see him. Maybe

Mr Perkins had also mentioned the photograph he'd shown me. Well, actually I was glad. I'd rather have this all out in the open . . .

This conversation was raging so loudly in my head, I stopped listening to Grandad for a few seconds. When I tuned in again, I realized that he wasn't talking about Mr Perkins at all. Instead, he was telling me about the council wanting to put up a little statue of him outside the new village hall. It would be of him during his days as a Spitfire ace.

'It just doesn't seem right somehow,' said Grandad quietly.

'Why not?' I asked.

'We were pilots, not heroes. Churchill pushed us into the public eye . . . but we were just doing a job, really. If they remember anyone, it should be all those who never came home.'

'They won't do that, though. If the statue's not of you, it'll be of some mouldy old mayor from the 1860s.'

'Who's got as much right to be up there as me.'

'I don't agree. I think it should be of you.' I went on, 'Your statue will remind people like me of all the sacrifices your generation made. And we need reminding.'

Grandad sat, thinking about what I'd said. 'So if I agree to this, I'm not a vain old man snatching the glory from his dead comrades?'

'No, because you're always talking about them, you keep their memory alive. And so will the statue.'

Then Grandad spotted Nan coming back. He sprang

up. 'I haven't told your nan about this yet. I wanted to get your opinion first.'

So in this matter he'd ranked my opinion as the most crucial. I can't tell you how good that made me feel.

'But don't let on,' he hissed. 'And when I tell you both about the statue, look very surprised, all right?'

'All right.' We grinned conspiratorially at each other.

Later that evening, Mum came over as well. And the four of us drank a toast to what I called 'Grandad's New Career as a Statue'. It was a great moment – until a fifth person came in. No one else saw him arrive, but I couldn't miss him.

He planted his feet in front of Grandad and wouldn't go away. It was as if he'd been summoned up. And now, every time I looked at Grandad, there he was too: Grandad's teenage self, in a Blackshirt uniform.

I couldn't get him to leave either. So in the end *I* had to go. I pretended I had too much homework to stay any longer. 'The teachers will kill me for saying this,' said Grandad, 'but I wish they'd give you all a little more time to dream.'

Next day too I stayed away from Grandad. I knew if I went round, that other figure would only start haunting me again.

Then on Saturday morning Grandad rang and invited me to go out for a walk with Gertie and him. And I couldn't get out of that.

Grandad lived right on the edge of the village. After

his cottage, there was just the local church, then a stream and a meadow where you could find very tame horses galloping about. And it was his favourite walk, because if he ventured into the centre of the village he was always getting stopped by someone, and that can get a little wearing.

Today he was in especially high spirits. The news about the statue seemed to have rejuvenated him. 'Smell that air,' he said. 'Spring is on its way. Soon there'll be blossom and birdsong . . .'

Then he started quizzing me about the names of trees and plants. When I first arrived here, he'd been shocked by my ignorance, so he began teaching me about them. And every so often he'd give me a surprise test, like today.

It was all very light-hearted. And normally I enjoyed it. But today I was too distracted to really join in, for *he* was here again. I didn't think I'd be able to see him in the daylight, but I could. He was in black and white, but he was here all right, like Grandad's evil shadow. He'd escaped out of the past, and I knew he'd never return until I . . .

I don't really want to tell you the next thing I did. I think you'll find it hard to understand. So let me try and explain something.

At the time, something inside me said I had no choice. I just had to do it. There really was no alternative. No other way out.

What triggered it was Grandad asking me about my book and when did I want to interview him again?

And I yearned to soar off into those wartime stories as

much as he did. But right now I was caught up in another story, about the Blackshirts and Mr Perkins, and I was so desperate to leave it, but the only way – THE ONLY WAY – was by asking Grandad . . .

But I did build up to it. I didn't just ask him outright, or anything. First of all, I said, 'Can we go back a bit further than your days in the RAF? I just wondered if you'd been in any boys' organizations like . . . well, the Scouts, for instance.'

'The Scouts,' said Grandad, all bright and twinkly. 'Do you know, I was, but not for very long. Can't remember why not. Yes I can. Hated the Scoutmaster.' He chuckled. I tried to laugh too. 'Do you want to know any more about my brief, very inglorious, scouting career?' he asked.

'No, no, that's great. How about the Boys' Brigade? That was big in the 1930s.'

'I used to see them marching about, banging a drum, and I thought, that looks like fun, but I never joined them,' said Grandad.

'And did you have the army cadets . . .?'

'Way back then?' teased Grandad. 'Not sure; I don't think so. We did have electricity, though.' He laughed. And I thought, leave it now, Grandad's so happy. Don't spoil the mood. Change the subject. But that voice inside me said I had to press on. Things would never be right between Grandad and me until I did ask him . . .

'And then there was another organization –' my heart was pounding so hard I could hear it in my ears – 'called the Blackshirts. Were you ever in the Blackshirts?'

At once Grandad looked not just shocked, but really,

really shocked, as if a comet or something had just shot past us. He turned away from me and looked over at Gertie, who was off the lead for a few minutes and was barking happily at nothing in particular.

'No,' he said slowly, 'I was never in that one.' He looked back at me.

'Not even for a couple of weeks?'

He flinched at my persistence. 'Not even for a couple of hours,' he said firmly.

And that was such a big, fat lie, I felt as if I'd just been kicked in the stomach.

'Sorry, I can't be more helpful.' All of a sudden his voice was hoarse, but there was steel in it too, as if he were closing down that line of questioning once and for all.

But he hadn't.

I couldn't see that other figure any more, that ghost from Grandad's past. But I could still sense him hovering between us.

Grandad's pretending was no defence against him.

We chatted together about other things – but in a fairly half-hearted way. The walk back seemed to last for ages too. I was quite relieved when we reached Grandad's house. I was following him inside for a cup of tea and a hot scone – an absolute ritual, every time we came back from a walk. Only today Grandad said, 'Do you mind if I don't ask you in . . . feeling a bit groggy. Must have been overdoing it.'

He did look suddenly older and very weary. I thought, have I done this to him? Was it my questioning that made him ill?

'Shall I come in with you and make you a drink . . .?'
I began.

'No, no,' said Grandad, closing the door on me, 'I'll be
just fine after a little rest.'

I felt really awful after that. Grandad was the very last
person I'd ever want to hurt. He meant the world to me.
But he had also lied twice to me. Twice. Whopping great
lies, which just pushed me away from him.

I didn't know what to do next. So in the end I rang
Yolande and she suggested meeting on the common.

Right from the start she seemed edgy and strained. But
she said that everything was all right. Anyway, we sat on
the grass – the place was deserted apart from a few boys
playing football – and I told her about this morning.

After I'd finished, she said quietly, 'Last Christmas I
met up with a girl I'd known at primary school. She'd
moved away and we lost touch, until she turned up here
again for a visit. And she had a real go at me. She said
I'd excluded her from things and made her feel like a total
outcast.'

'That doesn't sound like you,' I said.

'Oh, I'm not that nice,' Yolande admitted. 'But in her
case I really don't remember doing any of that. But she's
convinced I did. So who's right?' She shrugged her
shoulders. 'Do you see what I'm saying? Memories aren't
clear and definite – they're wobbly, slippery things. And
often you can never really get hold of what happened . . .'

I nodded. 'Yes, I see that.'

'So Mr Perkins acts as if he and your grandad were

great mates. Your grandad can't remember him at all. Does it really matter?'

'It wouldn't matter at all,' I replied, 'if I hadn't seen that photograph.'

She groaned. 'Oh no. You're obsessed with that.'

'No, I'm not.'

'You are, Charlie.' Her voice rose. 'And it's starting to get on my nerves actually.'

'Oh, right,' I said in a hurt kind of way. 'Sorry about that.' But I had to add, 'That photo proves Grandad was in the Blackshirts for a bit anyway . . . so he can't have forgotten that.'

'All right, maybe he hasn't – but so what,' said Yolande. 'He made one mistake that he wants to keep private. Isn't he entitled to do that?' She didn't wait for me to answer. 'You seem to think you can just burrow around in any part of your grandad's life – well, you can't. I really believe you're trespassing.' She practically screamed that last word at me.

The boys playing football stopped to look at us. They thought we were having a lovers' tiff. If only. I didn't understand why she was getting so heated over this. In fact, I wished I'd never started this conversation. So I said quietly, 'Let's talk about something else.'

'Not until you've answered my question,' she hissed. 'Hasn't your grandad got a right to privacy?'

'Of course he has.' All at once I was getting annoyed too. 'Look, I'm not discussing this with you any more.'

There was silence for a moment until she burst out, 'I know, why don't you tie your grandad to a chair, shine a torch in his face and say, "Are you now, or have you ever been, a fascist?" That should settle all your suspicions once and for all.'

'Thanks so much for that,' I replied through clenched teeth. 'You've been incredibly helpful.'

'You want some advice?' she began.

'No, I don't, actually.'

'Well, you're getting some,' she yelled, causing the boys to pause for a second time in their game of football. 'Forget all about that stupid photo and creepy Mr Perkins and just have some faith in your grandad!'

Then she jumped up and stormed off to the accompaniment of the boys chanting, 'Trouble. Trouble. Trouble.'

I didn't go after her.

I just sat there, thinking how today had been like one of those dreams where everything becomes confused and strange. And you find yourself going deeper and deeper into a world you hardly recognize.

Chapter Fifteen

After that, things got even weirder.

I went round to Grandad's as usual. And there we were, talking and smiling and being ever so polite to each other and pretending everything was all right. But it wasn't.

It was as if there were an invisible wall all round him that night. I just couldn't get near him. The grandad I knew was a million miles away from me. And I didn't know what to do to bring him back.

Finally I said that I had to interview him again for the book. But even that failed. Grandad just nodded solemnly and said, 'If you like, Charlie,' in such a dead voice, it sent a chill right through me.

Still, I pressed on. I said I'd be round tomorrow with my tape recorder.

Only, the next night, it was Nan who opened the door. 'I'm afraid he's feeling so tired he'll have to postpone his interview. I think he wants to save his energy for

Thursday.' (That was the first night of the play Mum was directing.) 'But come in and have a cup of tea, love.'

'No, you're all right, Nan,' I muttered. 'See you soon.'

And at that moment I knew how very serious things were. Grandad said that talking to me always made him feel better. And he loved being interviewed. He'd never have turned down one of those interviews just to go to bed early.

The truth was, Grandad didn't want to see me.

And all because of one little question: 'Were you ever in the Blackshirts?'

What had I done?

If I could un-ask that question now, I would. What is it they say in the courtrooms: 'Strike that remark from the records.' Well, that's what I wanted to do: scratch out that question, erase it forever.

But I couldn't.

That question was now there in Grandad's head – and, to be honest, in mine as well. I had other questions too.

What on earth was Grandad doing in the Blackshirts? Hadn't he realized it was a fascist organization? And why had he lied to me?

These questions just kept creeping back. They were unstoppable.

It was strange, really: the past was the thing that had brought Grandad and me together. Now it was pushing us away from each other. If only I hadn't started nosing about in Grandad's past. I suppose I got the bug after Geoff. Grandad had been so thrilled by that reunion. I had just thought I'd try and create some more magic, by bringing back other figures from his faraway past.

But, just as archaeologists don't know what they're going to find when they start digging around – how was I to know I'd unearth Mr Perkins? Immediately I could picture him, leering at me. He'd goaded me into asking Grandad about the Blackshirts, hadn't he? He'd set me up.

Now the very best part of my life was falling to pieces and I hadn't a clue what to do about it.

I sat on the common for ages. I nearly rang Yolande. But, after the way she'd blown up last time, I decided not to bother her. I was worried about her, actually. I had a feeling she was in a bit of a state. But I was also pretty certain it was because of Callum – and her unrequited love for him. And I just couldn't bear to hear about that. Not right now.

I got home just after nine o'clock. Mum was still away at her rehearsal. I went upstairs to my bedroom, then I spotted a letter propped up against my hairbrush. Mum must have put it up there earlier.

I don't often get letters, so I looked at it curiously for a moment. When I opened it, a newspaper cutting fell out. I picked it up. It was an article about a statue of Grandad going up. There'd been a long piece in our local paper about it, and this was a slightly edited version. But who could have sent it to me? I suppose I should have guessed. The letter said:

Delighted to see this (enclosed). I have so enjoyed our journeys down memory lane. Hope it's been useful for your book. Remember me to your grandfather.

Kind regards, Maurice Perkins.

Anyone seeing it would just think it was a bland little note from a dear old gentleman. They wouldn't know the total havoc he had caused. And it was as if there were no getting away from him. He'd tracked me down here (I certainly hadn't given him my address) and sent this smug, gloating letter.

'Hope it's been useful.' He knew exactly how useful his reminiscences had been.

I tore that letter into smaller and smaller pieces – as well as the cutting. I didn't want to touch anything that had been contaminated by him. Yet even then Mr Perkins still hung over Grandad and me like a dark, toxic cloud.

I could see Mr Perkins in the Blackshirts all right, just revelling in all the trouble they caused. And he was still stirring things up now, he and his family. I mean, what harm have the asylum seekers ever done to him, but he's holding that meeting at his house tomorrow to . . .

And then, quite suddenly, an idea just sort of brushed against me. I'd felt so powerless lately. And I hated feeling like that. But here was something I could do.

I sat down and thought some more.

Then I picked up my mobile and dialled Mr Perkins's number.

Chapter Sixteen

I gave my best ever acting performance on the phone to Mr Perkins. I was careful not to overplay my part either. I just told him how I'd been avidly reading everything I could find about the Blackshirts (this part was true anyhow) and that I understood them much better now.

'They just wanted to make Britain great again, didn't they?' I said.

I could hear the excitement gathering in Mr Perkins. 'That's right. We acted out of a love for Britain and a desire for it to be reborn as a truly important country once more . . .'

He kept me talking for ages and even told me about some other websites I might care to visit. He was chuffed to bits that he'd hooked in a fresh young convert.

Then I asked very casually about the meeting at his house tomorrow. I said that Grandad wouldn't be well enough to attend, but I'd be most interested in coming along.

My request was granted right away. Mr Perkins added, 'We shall be looking for some helpers to distribute leaflets . . .'

'I'd be honoured to help.'

Afterwards I did a little dance of triumph. I'd managed to trick my way into this little nest of fascists with surprising ease.

So far, so good.

My bike had been playing up since my accident on my last visit to Mr Perkins, so I decided to get the bus this time. I found out there was one just after six o'clock, which would be ideal. I was too nervous to eat much of the meal that Mum had left for me (her final rehearsal tonight) and I was just getting ready to leave when my mobile rang. It was Yolande.

Immediately my heart started jumping about a bit.

'I'm so very sorry,' she was speaking very quickly. 'You must have thought I was a total cow on Saturday.'

I laughed in a 'perish the thought' sort of way.

'It wasn't you I was mad at, at all. It was someone else.' Immediately I thought of Callum and felt a little stab of jealousy.

'So, sorry again – and how are you?' she asked.

'Very pleased you rang.'

'How about meeting up tonight?'

'I'm afraid I'm going out.'

'Oh, OK.'

But I didn't think she believed me, so I blurted out, 'I'm seeing Mr Perkins actually.'

A sharp intake of breath. 'Why are you seeing that

creep? And that's not meant to be a criticism,' she added hastily. 'It's just, do you really want to see him again so soon?'

'Tonight's different,' I explained. 'You know his son's standing as our I-hate-asylum-seekers MP. Well, he's holding that meeting at his dad's house tonight for the action group – and I'm going to sabotage it.'

There was a stunned silence for a moment before Yolande asked, 'How exactly are you going to do that?'

'By standing up and arguing with him.'

'That's incredibly brave of you.'

I really liked her saying that.

'So who's going to be there?' she went on.

'Not sure, exactly,' I said. 'Some elderly racists . . .'

'And some scabby-looking young ones with skinhead haircuts too, I expect.' Before I could reply, she went on, 'I sort of wish I could go with you. But they'd never allow a black person into their hallowed meeting. Not that they're racist or anything.'

'Oh, never.' I laughed.

'Still, when people fought duels, didn't they always have seconds to hold their coats and clean up all the messy blood afterwards? Well, I could be your second if you like. I'll just come along and wait for you somewhere.'

I hadn't been expecting this at all. 'Would you really want to just hang about?'

'Well, I'm not doing anything else . . .'

And, in fact, she was waiting at the bus stop before I got there. She called out: 'Heroes shouldn't be leaving on the bus. You should be charging off on a white steed.'

'Ah, but they're all out of white steeds tonight. I checked.'

'They do get very booked up.' She laughed, then slipped her hand in mine just as if we were setting off on a date. Then she whispered, 'I really admire what you're doing,' as if I were someone who cared deeply about the rights of asylum seekers and spoke out regularly against racism, when actually the main reason I was going was because I was mad at Perkins for smashing up my life – and this was the only way I could get back at him. I was doing a good thing for not such good reasons, I suppose.

The bus was incredibly slow. But Yolande and I chatted away, making everything seem oddly unreal. At the end of this journey was I really going to face Mr Perkins once more?

But the bus finally shuddered to a halt at the top of his road.

'There's a little cafe round the corner,' I began.

'I noticed it,' said Yolande. 'I'll wait there for you.' Then she leant right into me and kissed me on my cheek. OK, that wasn't exactly what I wanted, but I still felt like the knight being embraced by the fair maiden just before he charges into battle. As I was going, Yolande whispered to me, 'Don't be too brave.' That made it sound as if I were doing something really dangerous.

Still, when I stood outside Mr Perkins's house again I remembered going up into that shiver-some room and seeing the photograph – it all came back. Did I really want to go back there again? But then I pictured what a shock I was going to give Mr Perkins tonight. That fuelled me.

I rang the doorbell. It was answered by a sour-looking woman who stared at me suspiciously. Somehow I felt she could tell I wasn't a true supporter. But then Mr Perkins tottered forward in a cream-coloured suit and a purple bow tie.

'Welcome, young man,' he purred. 'This is Charlie,' he said to the sour-faced old woman. 'The grandson of an old school friend of mine, and he's interested in what we have to say and has even volunteered to help. That's right, isn't it?'

'It really is,' I said.

'May I introduce Belinda, my daughter-in-law.'

The sour-faced woman gave me a thin, tight smile. 'Your support is appreciated.' She was still looking at me doubtfully, though.

Then Mr Perkins told me we were meeting up in the attic. So I climbed up two flights of stairs and stepped into a surprisingly large room.

A model railway track stretched right round the walls and even over the door. There were also pictures of steam trains idyllically puffing their way through the countryside. Tonight, though, blown-up newspaper articles about asylum seekers were slapped up beside them, and the headlines were like someone shouting in your face.

About thirty chairs had been set out, while at the back of the room were cups for tea and coffee, and plates crammed with cakes. In the background, classical music was playing. It was all so genteel and respectable: a pot of tea, a home-made cake and a large helping of racism.

A man in an expensive blue suit came over to me. He gleamed like someone off to a job interview; even his shoes had been polished like glass. His hair was a glossy golden colour and his eyes were eager and alert. 'Hello, I'm Gerald Perkins.' He said his name confidingly, as if he were delivering a secret password.

'I'm Charlie, my grandfather knew Mr Perkins at school –'

'But how fascinating,' he interrupted. 'Thanks for taking the trouble to come along tonight. And I don't mind admitting, Charlie, I'm mildly petrified about it all.' He talked fast and smiled almost the entire time. 'Tell me, how is your grandfather, Charlie?'

I started answering him, but his eyes were already roaming around the rest of the room. He suddenly patted my hand and said, 'We must talk more later.' Then he was off to greet a woman wearing yellow-tinted glasses the size of car headlamps.

I went over to the food table. There were glasses of wine too, so I helped myself to one. A massive, bald man was wolfing down a plateful of cakes, and not quietly either. He nodded at me while another couple stood sipping their wine as if it were vile medicine. An air of despair hung over them both.

After he'd finished eating his food, the massive, bald man lumbered over to me. He appeared to be dressed entirely in 1970s leisurewear. He placed a huge hand on my shoulder.

'You have been observed,' he said solemnly. 'And unless you leave quietly I shall report you to the authorities.'

'For what?' I gasped.

'Drinking under age, aren't you?' Then he chuckled loudly. 'Only messing. I'm Fred, who the hell are you?'

'Charlie.'

'Well, as you can see, Charlie, I'm not backward in coming forward. If I see someone looking a bit lonely, I go up and talk to them.'

I tried my best to look grateful. Then he lowered his voice. 'These immigrants are crucifying us, aren't they? I mean, I'm a very compassionate person, but enough is enough. It's time the people in power heard what we had to say . . .'

I was spared any more of his reflections by a loud, squawking noise; it sounded as if a parrot had escaped. In fact it was an ancient, heavily made-up lady who screeched, 'Why are we meeting all the way up here? Have some consideration for the elderly.'

'We just thought it would be more comfortable,' explained Mr Perkins Senior, panting slightly as he tottered into view. A crowd of people was surging in behind him. They all had a pent-up look as if they were already at the end of their tether with life. And none looked under forty – except, that is, for one person, who I recognized instantly.

Raymond.

The boy I'd nearly run over. I'd just never have suspected him of being in on this. I felt oddly disappointed, even though I hardly knew him. I looked at him, but he didn't acknowledge me. He chatted away with Fred in a very pally manner, though.

Then Mr Perkins started clapping his hands, saying it was half past seven so could we make a start.

'This is a select meeting for our action group,' said Mr Perkins in his treacly voice. 'It's such a pleasure to welcome you all.' He waved a hand at all the people perched on tiny chairs. 'This is a very exciting evening for me . . .'

You don't know just how exciting, I thought.

Chapter Seventeen

I'd worked out exactly what I was going to do.

I'd let Gerald Perkins burble on for a bit, while I made notes. Then I'd jump up, just like a lawyer in court, and pull all his arguments to pieces. I'd do it really calmly and forensically – but I'd be deadly just the same – demolishing all his racist ravings forever.

Gerald Perkins stood in front of a table. On it was a large flag of St George and an equally large framed picture of him with his wife, looking as miserable as ever, and a girl in pigtails. I think we were all supposed to go, 'Aaah,' and declare, 'Now I've seen that yukky family snap I'll follow him anywhere.' He said, 'First I just want to pay tribute to my father. He fought in a war to save us – and our culture.' Applause started up. 'And he brought me up with proper English values. Thanks, Dad.' Even louder applause now, while 'Dad' bowed and smirked.

Now here it comes, I thought, all the lies about asylum

seekers. But instead he waffled on some more about England and how glad he was to have grown up when the spirit of England was still alive. Then he started talking about the local post office closing down and how you had to go miles and miles for most hospital operations now. 'I don't think that's right, do you?' he demanded.

'No,' murmured a few voices.

'Can't hear you,' he cried, just as if he were in a pantomime. 'Do you think that's right?'

And just like kids at a pantomime, they all roared back, 'No!' Fred's voice yelling out above everyone else's.

Gerald Perkins went on for ages about all the local problems, with people calling out extra comments too. There was a kind of humming fury throughout the room now. 'But the people in power never, ever notice us, do they?'

The audience yelled back, 'No,' and very unwillingly I had to concede that he was right on that point.

Take the Iraq war: everyone at my school was against that – teachers and pupils – we signed petitions, even went to a massive rally in London that was attended by over two hundred thousand people. And I thought, they've got to respond to this. But they didn't. The war in Iraq wasn't delayed one second despite all our protests.

'I'm sick of being ignored, aren't you?' cried Mr Perkins.

A thunderous chorus of 'Yes' by everyone – even me. Yes, for a few seconds there, he'd caught me. And I too was full of rage at my own powerlessness.

But then he started talking about the disused office being used as a centre for asylum seekers. 'Our hard-earned taxes are being spent housing total strangers in the kind of luxury we can't afford for ourselves. We can't afford hospital beds but we can afford to have waves of asylum seekers swamping us.'

Tremendous applause broke out now. Then people were shouting out, 'They just come here, do nothing and get in the queue first,' while the old, heavily made-up woman had gone totally off her rocker yelling, 'We'll be having riots in the streets! And muggings!'

And how cleverly Gerald Perkins had linked everyone's feelings of frustration and powerlessness with the arrival of the asylum seekers. Somehow they were to blame for everything that had gone wrong in people's lives, although they hadn't even arrived yet.

Find a group of outsiders and lay everything you can think of at their feet. Scapegoat them for it all. Well, it worked for Hitler, didn't it, when he blamed all Germany's problems on the Jews and immigrants? Oswald Mosley tried something very similar.

Did Grandad join in any of that? Did he allow himself to get all whipped up with hatred?

I just couldn't think about that at the moment. Instead, I made detailed notes, my pen racing across the page. Any moment now I would stand up and demolish all these arguments. I'd show them they couldn't pin all their problems on to the poor asylum seekers: stop them coming and everything will be wonderful – I don't think so.

But I wouldn't get worked up. I'd be very reasonable. Gerald Perkins had been careful to wrap the nastiness and prejudice of his rant in consoling phrases about England. Well, I was going to unpick all that as well.

Now he was saying how all political parties had been thoroughly discredited. You couldn't trust any of them. The only way forward was through independent candidates fighting on single issues. 'And I promise you,' he cried, his voice suddenly hoarse with emotion, 'I will fight this centre for asylum seekers with every fibre of my being.'

People were standing up and applauding now. He raised his hand. 'Save your energy for the rally we're organizing to launch my campaign on Saturday . . .'

They were mad with fervour now. Raymond was leaning so far forward, he was almost jumping out of his chair. Definitely time to speak up. So, my heart booming away, I whispered, 'This is for you, Grandad.'

Then, just as I was about to start, someone burst into the meeting yelling, 'I'm from the Greenshirts. We believe in peace and tolerance. Anyone want to join me?'

I whirled round and saw – Yolande.

Chapter Eighteen

A shocked hush fell over the entire room. People gaped at Yolande in slack-jawed amazement, unable to say anything. They were totally transfixed. So what should I do? Should I go over to her? And why on earth had she done this?

'I'm sorry, young lady,' Gerald Perkins's voice sliced through the silence, crisp and confident, 'but we really can't help you.' He made it sound as if she'd popped in to ask for directions. 'My wife will show you out.' Belinda Perkins was standing right behind Yolande now and looking even more grim-faced than usual.

'So you don't wish to join the Greenshirts?' asked Yolande.

'Actually,' he said, 'this is a private meeting and you're on private property, and I'm afraid I must insist you leave now.' Then he waved his hand, as if dismissing her. That little gesture inflamed me. How dare he treat Yolande with so little respect.

Almost without realizing it I was on my feet. Then it was all very odd: my head felt as if it were floating far above the rest of my body. I knew that it was just my nerves kicking in. But I'd been long enough preparing what I was going to say. I'd be fine, once I got started. Then Yolande and I could leave this hellhole in triumph.

'Ladies and gentlemen, you mustn't allow yourselves to be lured into racism and fascism.' That was the sum total of everything I managed to say before I was interrupted by something flashing through the air like a firework. It hit Gerald Perkins smack on the cheek. Then it exploded.

Gerald Perkins's face was covered in what looked like blood. It was spreading furiously too. His shirt, his suit – it was everywhere. Only it wasn't blood: it was red dye. And what had erupted over Gerald Perkins was, in fact, a water bomb. So it was nothing really – just like having a custard pie slapped in your face.

Even so, Gerald Perkins was very shocked. He swayed back for a moment, clawing at the air like a monster out of an old horror film. And who had thrown that water bomb? For a wild second I thought it was Yolande. But in fact the culprit had been . . . Raymond.

He yelled: 'All of you are nothing but Hitler lovers!' A kind of gigantic shiver ran through the room.

But then people were on their feet, shouting at Raymond and Yolande – and at me too. 'Can't someone control these punks?' bellowed Fred, whose face had turned all twisted and nasty. I caught the full force of one of his grimaces.

I immediately rushed over and stood beside Yolande.

Fred worried me a lot. I felt that he could turn extremely violent at any moment. 'You're certainly full of surprises,' I murmured to Yolande. She just smiled and took my hand. We felt each other shuddering. So much seemed to have happened in these last few minutes. And at the back of my mind I was thinking: what next?

Mr Perkins Senior staggered to his feet. But it was his son who took charge again, 'blood' still glistening on his chin. He cried exultantly, 'There you see, ladies and gentlemen, clear evidence of the total breakdown of our society. Lawlessness now rules.' The audience roared their agreement. He pointed at Raymond. 'I must ask you and your fellow agitators to leave this house now, without causing any more harm. If you do not do so immediately I shall call the police.'

'Call them anyway,' cried Fred.

'It's all right, we're leaving,' Raymond announced, as if he were our ringleader. 'But we'll be back to stop you at every turn. Wherever you look, we'll be right behind you. You will never succeed.'

With that he walked over to Yolande and me, and the three of us thudded down the stairs with Gerald Perkins's wife right behind us.

At the door she hissed, 'Do you have any idea of all the distress you've caused tonight?'

'Oh, we're total amateurs compared to you,' replied Raymond in such a solemn tone, even she was taken aback.

Outside I gave Yolande a hug.

'So you two know each other, then?' said Raymond.

'Her face is mildly familiar,' I said. 'In fact, she reminds me of someone I left waiting for me at the cafe.'

Yolande laughed in an embarrassed way. And then we heard this voice boom, 'You're not getting away with that, you know.'

The next thing I knew, Fred was hurtling towards us like some exploding firestorm. 'When he gets mad, he totally loses it,' whispered Raymond. Then he added, 'Run.'

But we already were. We pelted down that road, but Fred was catching us up. I took one quick glance at him. He was running with his arms out, and his eyes were bulging with hatred.

Then another voice called, 'Fred, don't descend to their level.' It was Gerald Perkins. A moment later he yelled, 'Fred – stop now!' He could have been giving instructions to a disobedient child.

And Fred did as he was told, even if he did holler after us, 'I know where you live, you haven't heard the end of this.'

The three of us stood, doubled up, trying to get our breath back. We decided to 'de-brief', as Raymond put it, in the cafe.

The boy behind the counter gave us a weary grimace. He took off his headphones and handed us each a menu. 'Back again,' he said to Yolande.

'It must be the wonderful atmosphere,' she replied. Apart from us, the place was completely empty.

'I thought I was a lone sniper there tonight,' said Raymond. He had a way of saying quite dramatic things in a very deadpan, expressionless way. 'So tell me, how did you get on to them?'

'Well, my grandad was at school with old Mr Perkins. I was interviewing him when I found out about his son's activities.' Then, keen to change the subject, I asked, 'How about you, then?'

'Fred's a neighbour of mine –' he said.

'So he really does know where you live,' cut in Yolande.

'Oh yes.' He shrugged.

'So you'll have to watch your back for a bit,' said Yolande.

'That just comes with the territory, when you're challenging fascists,' he said airily. 'I heard Fred mouthing off about this amazing new politician who was going to get rid of all the asylum seekers. So I pretended to be interested . . . We thought it would be best if I went to the meeting alone tonight.'

'We?' I asked.

'Yeah, the Fighters Against Fascism. We're a new organization. You could say we're fighting people's apathy as well, because they think they can just ignore all this. But they can't. If we don't challenge it, we could all wake up one day in a much nastier world.' He looked suddenly desolate. 'I don't understand why people can't see that.'

'Have you got many people in your organization?' asked Yolande.

'Just five at the moment . . . and I'm the leader,' Raymond added proudly. 'Opposing Perkins is our first major campaign. He's not to be underestimated either.' He turned to me. 'Sorry for interrupting your speech, only

101

I saw a perfect opportunity for a hit. Anyway, you were wasting your time; you can't reason with people who think in such a warped manner. They've just got to be stamped out straight away, so they don't get a chance to spread their poison.'

He made them sound as if they were the carriers of some terrible virus. But weren't at least some of them just frightened, gullible – and miserable? I'd never seen so many deeply gloomy people gathered in one room before. And wasn't there something a bit fascistic about not even allowing them to spout their views, however repellent? I wasn't quite sure about that. But I did feel cheated that I hadn't had the chance to expose Gerald Perkins's arguments verbally. Throwing water bombs did make a dramatic point, I suppose. But that wasn't going to change anyone's mind. While a good argument just might.

'The far right is on the rise, you know,' said Raymond. 'And racism is too.' He turned to Yolande. 'But I expect you've had some experience of that, haven't you?'

That question took her totally by surprise. And me. It seemed a bit personal as well, especially coming from someone Yolande hardly knew. Only Raymond looked so serious and concerned, as if he were a police officer asking it, that Yolande didn't take offence.

She said, 'Well, I don't think people around here have met that many black people. And when we first moved here, it was like all they could see was that I was a different colour to them. Everything else about me was irrelevant. And that was pretty annoying.'

Raymond nodded, completely absorbed by what Yolande was saying.

'In the past a few people would call out things, and that got me down a bit. But most people aren't like that at all. And I try not to think too much about the negative side of things.' She suddenly beamed one of her amazing smiles at Raymond. And for a moment all his intense seriousness fell away from him and he was just a shy schoolboy who'd been smiled at by a very pretty girl. He even smiled back at her.

Then his mobile rang. 'It's the other members,' he explained. 'They want a full report on what happened tonight, so I shall have to go. But we'll need everyone we can muster, to be at Perkins's rally on Saturday at five. So try and make it. We'll keep in contact anyhow.' Then he wrote down Yolande's and my phone numbers and handed round his cards with FIGHTERS AGAINST FASCISM in huge letters. Underneath was his name, his title – Leader and Coordinator – followed by his phone number and email address.

As he was leaving, he said, 'Please be very careful these cards don't fall into the wrong hands,' in such a grave voice, Yolande and I nearly burst out laughing.

After he'd gone, Yolande told me why she'd gatecrashed Perkins's meeting. 'I was sitting here in this ghastly cafe, and time was passing so slowly – and I kept imagining the people at the meeting: all these mean, nasty lads with big boots and swastika tattoos . . .'

I grinned.

'And I thought, if Charlie speaks out they'll kick him

to death in an instant. So I decided there was nothing for it, I'd have to do my Wonder Woman bit and rescue him.'

We were both grinning now.

'I was standing outside Perkins's house, plucking up my courage, when a woman came out.'

'Hatchet face?'

'That's her. And she asked in this very snooty voice, "Can I help you?" So that's when I burst out, "Yes, I've got this message for Charlie Marriott from his family. And it's absolutely and completely urgent. So where is he?" Well, she told me, and then I just rocketed up those stairs with her following me, all suspiciously. Then I dived into that meeting and just said the very first thing that came into my head. The Greenshirts actually exist, you know. Their motto is "Span the world with friendship". And they believe in peace, like me.' She paused for a moment. 'Of course, then I saw how very much you needed rescuing from that army of blue rinses . . .' She suddenly started laughing, and her loud, infectious laugh just soared out over that dreary cafe.

Then she looked at me. And it was nothing, just a glance. But it was like an electric shock ripping through me. I promise you, I'm not exaggerating. That really is the only way I can describe it. And I was sure Yolande had felt it too. In fact, I'd have bet my life on it. That's how certain I was.

So then I said in a surprisingly cool manner (I'm not often cool, but for a few seconds I really was then), 'Once when I asked you out, you turned me down. Don't miss your chance a second time.'

I thought she might laugh or smile at least. But she didn't. Instead, she looked away from me and said in this funny, muffled little voice, 'I told you why I couldn't go out with you.'

'I don't believe you.'

'Don't you?' Her voice seemed to be shrinking. And she sounded so miserable I wanted to reach out and hold her in my arms.

'Come on,' I said.

'What?' she whispered.

'Don't make my heart bleed for you any longer.'

She didn't answer for a moment. Then she said, in this soft, urgent voice, 'All right, Charlie, if you really want to know – I can't go out with you because I'm pregnant.'

Chapter Nineteen

Shock scrambled my brain.

I really hadn't been expecting Yolande to say that. In fact, I was knocked sideways. I tried to say something but couldn't find the words. Still, I couldn't just gape at her in silence. So in the end I babbled, 'Oh, right, well . . . congratulations.'

That was exactly the wrong thing to say.

'Congratulations,' she echoed disbelievingly.

Now she thought I was being sarcastic. And really I wasn't. But it was extremely difficult to know how to respond. I mean, you can't just say, 'Ah, how interesting,' or something. So then I asked, 'Have you told Callum?'

Another mistake. She was positively bristling now. 'He's nothing to me. So why on earth should I tell him?'

'Because he's the father of your baby' was the logical answer. But I didn't pursue that one. I didn't want to stand up for Callum anyway.

'So what did your mum and dad say?' was my next question.

'I haven't told a single person – apart from you,' replied Yolande.

I felt quite proud that she'd confided in me. She must really trust me. So I had to get to grips with this.

'Exactly how pregnant are you?'

She smiled.

I felt my face reddening. 'I mean, how many weeks is it?'

'Six,' she practically whispered. 'So it's a tiny little thing, as small as a bean – not really anything yet. That's what I keep telling myself anyway.'

'So what are you going to do? Are you going to keep it?' I made it sound like an unwelcome pet.

'How can I?' she asked, turning to me.

Well, I didn't know. I was totally out of my depth, to be honest. 'I'm sure you can get tons of leaflets about all this. So maybe read some of those, they'll help you to decide what to do.'

'I've already decided,' she said flatly. 'It can't be a part of me. Not yet. So they'll just dissolve it away and I'll have my life back again and everything will go back to normal, won't it?'

I didn't answer.

Her voice rose. 'Charlie, I don't even know who I am yet. How can I bring up a child as well? You can't ask me to do that.'

'No,' I murmured.

'So last Saturday I had a consultation at the early

pregnancy unit, and they said if I want a termination, well, the whole thing can be over and done within a day.'

'That is quick,' I said. Then I added, 'Did you go on your own?'

'Oh yes,' replied Yolande briskly. 'Then I went and saw you on the common.'

'And heard me going on and on about Grandad and the Blackshirts . . .'

'At least it took my mind off things . . . even if I was pretty foul to you.'

'So when are you going to tell your parents?' I asked.

'Never,' she said firmly.

I started in surprise.

'If I tell them, it'll only spoil their life too. They won't shout at me or anything, but they'll be so miserable and disappointed, which is much, much worse, actually.'

I nodded.

'And then they'll decide it's all their fault and beat themselves up for no reason. Why should I put them through all that?' Her voice fell away. 'I've been the stupid one. Not them. And I shall just have to take the consequences this Saturday.'

'Is that when the deed will be done?'

'That's right.'

I still felt that she shouldn't be going through this alone. I wished I could do something for her – and I didn't mean flinging about a few platitudes.

No, I wanted to really help her. I'd loved to have said, 'Yolande, I know of a private clinic in Switzerland. I'll fly you there, they'll look after you so well, and I shall come too . . .'

'Stop it.' Yolande's command brought me out of my daydream.

'What?' I asked.

'Stop looking so concerned.'

I smiled sheepishly. 'Sorry.'

'And will you do me a big, big favour?'

'Definitely.'

'Forget everything I just said. It wasn't fair of me to dump this on you. And I'm dealing with it. I really wish I hadn't told you now.'

'I do want to help,' I said.

'I don't need any help,' said Yolande. 'Honestly, it's all sorted. Just forget it. Now, what time is the next bus?' she asked in a high, tight voice.

We had to run for it, actually, as it was the last one that night.

The bus rattled and wheezed along. We chatted about tonight. And it was an OK conversation, but the easy, relaxed intimacy we had had before was gone.

It's odd, actually. Yolande had just told me her deepest secret. And you'd think that would have made us closer than ever. But, in fact, it didn't, as I knew Yolande really regretted telling me now.

That made me think I'd let her down.

I felt sad inside, and frustrated and defeated too. Yolande never wanted to go out with me. She saw me as a friend, one she needed really badly right now. I'd just been fooling myself with all the romantic stuff.

Charlie – the love-god.

I laughed bitterly to myself.

I walked Yolande to the top of her road. Neither of us said much now. Our heads were too thick with thoughts.

Then Yolande kissed me on the lips – but very lightly. She said, 'I really think you should forget about your grandad and the Blackshirts now. He obviously wants it kept secret – well, that is his right, isn't it?'

I nodded slowly.

'And what I told you.' She smiled faintly. 'We'll never talk about it again.'

She didn't wait for me to reply, just walked off while I stood watching her melt away into the darkness like a shadow.

Chapter Twenty

I thought about Yolande some more that night.

She wanted a good friend – well, at least I could be that. And she needed help with her problem. But what exactly could I do? I knew next to nothing. I was useless.

I could always get hold of some of those leaflets on pregnancy myself and read up on it. Still, Yolande seemed to have made up her mind. But was she right?

I just wished someone else knew, like her parents. I suppose I could always tell them secretly. Meet them in private . . . No, no, no!

What a truly awful, disgusting idea. If I did that, I'd be betraying Yolande's trust completely – and I'd have failed her completely as a friend. No, all I could do was stand by her.

Later, I remembered what Yolande had said about Grandad. And I decided she'd given me excellent advice. All right, I was disappointed that Grandad couldn't tell me the truth about him and the Blackshirts, but I'd just have to get over it.

More than anything, I wanted things between Grandad and me to go back to the way they were before.

Only it didn't work out like that.

Next day, after school, Nan rang me. Grandad had yet another hospital appointment and wouldn't be home until about half past five. When he got back, wouldn't it be a great surprise if he discovered the garden – his pride and joy – had been tidied up.

So I did all these jobs, like raking the moss off the lawn and mowing the grass, while Nan sat in a deckchair. 'This won't do,' she said. 'I ask you round to help and end up leaving it all to you.'

'Don't worry about it,' I said.

Nan was one of those people who were usually bustling about the whole time. But she did look quite tired today.

'I'll do jobs like this anytime,' I said. 'It's no problem at all.'

She stared round approvingly at what I'd done. 'This is really going to cheer Grandad up all right,' she said.

'Has he been depressed, then?' I asked.

'He hasn't been himself, that's for certain,' replied Nan. 'It's having to go to hospital so often. Well, you know how much he loathes them. It's made him very strained and tense.'

I bet me asking about the Blackshirts hadn't exactly lifted his spirits either.

Then Nan got up and announced that she'd sat back

long enough and was going to do some pruning. Only she couldn't find her new gardening gloves.

'They must still be upstairs with my other birthday presents,' she said.

'You got gardening gloves as a birthday present?' I cried.

'Oh, I asked for them,' replied Nan.

I volunteered to find them for her.

'Oh, thanks, love, I'm pretty certain they're in the top drawer of my dressing table.'

Only they weren't.

So I started searching through the other drawers. I was so intent on what I was doing – and making so much noise – I didn't hear anyone creep upstairs. It was only when a voice exclaimed, 'What on earth do you think you're doing?' that I whirled round to see Grandad staring at me and breathing furiously.

'Oh, hi, Grandad. I was just –' I began.

But he shouted over me, 'What right do you have to come in here and raid my room whenever you feel like it?' His eyes were scorched with fury and he looked as if he were about to hit me.

I felt myself stagger back away from him. Why had Grandad suddenly morphed into this raging madman? I struggled to speak, but shock had knocked all the breath out of me.

'You've no right to be in here!' he bellowed. 'Go on, get out of my bedroom!'

'Yes, all right, Grandad,' I croaked, and something in my voice seemed to calm him down. A look of perplexity settled over his face, as if he couldn't quite understand what had just happened either.

But I didn't stay any longer. Instead, I tore back to Nan, still sitting in a deckchair in the garden. 'I couldn't get your gloves, Nan,' I said. 'I was looking for them when Grandad chucked me out.'

'He did what?' quavered Nan, springing up.

'He was really mad with me.'

'It must be the medication he's on,' said Nan. 'He'd never talk like that to you normally, love. You know that.' Then she added, 'Where is he now?'

'Still upstairs I think. Anyway, I'm off. See you again sometime.'

I was out of that house in seconds. I felt sick to the pit of my stomach. It was such a horrible moment – and a totally unexpected one. Grandad had never acted like this before. In fact, I don't think I'd ever seen him shout at anyone before. No, I was sure I hadn't.

Still, if Grandad had acted like that because of his medication . . . well, that was no problem at all. But I was absolutely certain it was for a totally different reason.

Grandad thought I was searching his room. He thought I was looking for something to link him with the Blackshirts. A rush of horror ran through me. Did he really believe I'd sneak up to his bedroom and rifle through his stuff in order to try and find something incriminating? That would be such a sneaky, shabby thing to do. Not my style at all. Surely Grandad realized that.

And then I thought: what if he really did have something to hide? What if he had a souvenir of his fascist days tucked away in some deep, dark corner because deep down he was still a fascist?

The terrible ideas kept coming now. It was as if the floodgates had been opened and out they poured, growing wilder and wilder.

It was just one tiny question: were you ever in the Blackshirts? But that was enough to let in something weird and destructive. It was as if a malign spirit had been released and now it was hanging over Grandad and me all the time. And it was just making us both do and think things that weren't in our true character.

I called Yolande. I asked her how she was, and she went immediately on the defensive. 'I'm absolutely fine. Why shouldn't I be?' She was worried that I was going to mention the subject I'd promised never to talk about again.

I didn't tell her what had happened earlier at Grandad's; I figured she had enough to worry about. So we just chatted about Mum's play tonight and other stuff like that. We didn't talk for very long either.

A couple of minutes later, the phone rang. It was Grandad. His voice sounded so thick and hoarse I hardly recognized it at first. 'Your nan has explained everything to me. And I wanted to apologize most sincerely for shouting at you. I behaved in a totally unacceptable way.'

He sounded so formal, as if he were reading from a prepared statement. There wasn't an ounce of his usual sparkle and warmth either. In fact, listening to him apologizing was nearly as scary as him shouting at me.

115

'That's quite all right, Grandad. There's no need to apologize, just forget it.'

I was replying in the same dry, cold tones. In fact, we were conversing together like two daleks.

'Well, thank you for taking it so well, and we'll see you at about seven o'clock.'

That was when we were all meeting up to see Mum's play (Mum, of course, had already left) and suddenly I dreaded it.

Mum's play was a big success, earning three curtain calls. But I'd say that the best performance that evening was undoubtedly given by Grandad.

Being a local celebrity, he attracted quite a lot of attention when he went out. He did that night. He was just as charming and funny and lively as ever. You'd never have guessed anything was bothering him. In fact, I would say he was even friendlier than usual to everyone.

Then Mum and I went back to his house for a celebratory drink. He carried on being cheerful, which was great, except that I felt he was still performing.

I thought Nan seemed a bit jittery, though. And later in the evening I found out why. We were all in the sitting room – and we'd just toasted Mum's play – when Nan said, 'You won't believe what he's gone and done.'

'Don't talk about me as if I'm not here,' murmured Grandad.

Nan ignored this. 'He's told the local council he doesn't want that statue of himself to go up after all.'

'But why?' Mum and I chorused together.

'You tell them,' said Nan, looking at Grandad, 'because I can't make head or tail of what you're talking about.'

Grandad threw out the palms of his hands. 'I just don't think they want me littering up the place.' He was still talking with that 'ho, ho, ho' in his voice he had used when we were at the play, and it was starting to get on my nerves.

'I'm with Nan on this one,' I said. 'I don't know what you're on about either.'

Grandad looked at me. 'I think it's a super idea to have a statue put up of an airman from World War II. I just don't want *my* name plastered all over it. Far better if it's symbolic.'

'I don't agree,' I said. 'It'll mean much more if it's a real person.' Then I added in a lower voice, 'I thought we'd talked about this.'

'Well, now I've thought about it some more . . . and it's not for me.'

'But what's changed your mind?' asked Mum, looking very puzzled.

'I've been unhappy about it for a while actually,' said Grandad. 'I should never have agreed to it in the first place.' He glanced in my direction. 'Allowed myself to be talked into it when I shouldn't have done. Now let that be an end to it. There are far more important things to be talking about than that.'

'Well, I admit I'm disappointed,' said Mum. 'I was so looking forward to showing off about it.'

'You'll be directing plays in the West End before you know it,' replied Grandad, 'and have much better things to show off about than me.' He rubbed his hands together, waking up Gertie, who was dozing beside him. 'Now will you all stop looking so serious for goodness' sake.' Then he laughed.

Only I didn't believe that laugh for a moment. It was totally fake. He was pretending he wasn't bothered about the statue, but I knew differently. He'd been so excited when he first heard – and honoured too. What had really changed his mind? Normally I'd have known straight away, Grandad and I were that close. But now it was as if he'd pulled down the blinds and gone somewhere deep inside himself, somewhere where even I couldn't reach him.

Later, when Mum and Nan disappeared into the kitchen for a few minutes, I said to him, 'It's about time we got on with our interviews for my book. How about tomorrow night?'

Grandad lifted his head slowly as if it had become very heavy. Then, after a moment's silence, he said, 'You don't want to waste your time listening to me rattling on about ye olden days . . . You've been very patient and kind. But I think it's time you moved on to another, far more rewarding subject.' This was all said in that jolly Father-Christmas-in-his-grotto voice he'd assumed all evening, which made it all the more disturbing somehow.

I stared at him. 'So you want to abandon the book?'

'I don't want you to stop writing. You've got a real talent for that. Nurture that talent. Look after it.' His words were encouraging, but his tone was so distant it made my stomach turn over. He was talking more like a careers teacher than my grandad. 'But I think we should call it a day on our book. You don't mind, do you?'

What sort of question was that? I minded bitterly.

'You spend too much time with old crocks like me. I think you need some fresh blood, don't you?'

Fresh blood! What was he on about? I couldn't even answer him, just stared hard at the carpet.

Then he announced in a very loud voice, 'I shall leave you night birds now, as some of us need to catch up on our beauty sleep.'

I listened incredulously. Grandad never went to bed this early. In fact, he was often roaming about at one or two in the morning. Nan went upstairs to see if he was all right.

When she came down she murmured, 'He says he's dead beat. I think it's these hospital visits, they've really taken it out of him.'

But I knew it wasn't just that. It was me. Grandad couldn't bear even to be in the same room as me now. My head was still reeling from the way he'd just abandoned our book. I'd poured everything into that. We both had. It was something we shared. Our lives touched there.

For days now, I'd sensed Grandad and me moving further and further apart. But tonight I'd been dropped completely.

I'd have promised anything on earth to stop that happening.

Back in my bedroom. On my bedside table, some books with sections on the Blackshirts, which I'd found in the library. But I hadn't even opened them. Why should I want to know any more about them? Didn't I have enough images of Blackshirts flashing through my head?

But that night I did pick one up and I read all about the violence at rallies. If anyone dared to heckle Oswald Mosley while he was having one of his rants, he'd just stop and fold his arms. That was the signal for the Blackshirts to eject the heckler – usually with great violence.

There were reports of people leaving a rally with blood streaming down their faces and their clothes all in tatters. Sometimes five or six Blackshirts would launch themselves into one heckler, hitting and kicking him in the head, the stomach . . . they were quite merciless.

Grandad must have seen some of this. Maybe even joined in. Did he actually beat people up?

I slammed the book shut. My head was bursting with so many questions already. I didn't want any more.

I closed my eyes and wandered in and out of dreams about the Blackshirts: they were marching with their right arms thrust forward and they were crying, 'Heil Mosley.'

And right in the middle of them was Grandad. He was raising his fists as if he wanted to hit someone. And he was saying to me, 'Come on, Charlie, this is where we belong – join us.'

I tried to yell back, 'Never!' But I couldn't even whisper; my voice had gone. I was just opening and shutting my mouth like a goldfish. I was very glad when I woke up.

I put on the light. Immediately, all the photographs of Grandad on the wall jumped out at me.

There was Grandad, posing beside a Spitfire. Grandad standing with a group of pilots . . . Normally, if ever I was depressed, I could look at these pictures and just slip inside them. And afterwards I'd feel stronger and inspired and able to face things again.

But tonight the pictures just seemed dead and meaningless. They hadn't anything to do with me any more.

So that's why at three o'clock in the morning I tore down every single one of them.

I told myself he'd packed me away tonight, so now it was my turn to give him the boot. That made me feel better – for about four seconds.

Afterwards, I lay in bed, staring around at the bare, empty walls. And I realized something: I hadn't just lost Grandad tonight. I'd lost part of me too.

The very best part.

Chapter Twenty-one

Next day, Yolande called. She wanted a favour. Well, two favours, actually.

'Could you possibly come round and have tea at my house tonight and make polite conversation with my old dears? Do you think you could bear that?'

I thought I probably could. She went on to ask if I'd pretend that she and I were going to Cambridge tomorrow (accompanied by my mum). I was a bit slow on the uptake and started to ask her why on earth she wanted to tell her parents that. But then I got it. She needed to cover for her time at the clinic.

'So you really don't mind?' she asked.

'What's to mind?' I replied. I was pleased, actually. At least it would take my mind off my grandad for a bit.

I'd met Yolande's parents briefly, at a performance of *An Inspector Calls*. They'd seemed rather formal then. But that night they were good fun, especially Yolande's mum.

I could see where Yolande got her energy and humour from.

After the meal, when Yolande and I were on our own in the kitchen, she said, 'My parents think you're absolutely marvellous . . . "A lovely lad", they said.'

'I like them too . . . your mum's a riot.'

Yolande smiled faintly then hissed, 'I really hate going behind their backs, but what else can I do?'

'But one day,' I hissed back, 'when they find out . . .?'

'They'll never find out.'

'But just say, somehow they did. They'll feel really terrible.'

'So you think I should tell them then?' she demanded.

'I think I do. Yes,' I admitted. Especially now that I'd met them, I thought they deserved to know and be given a chance to help.

Yolande didn't reply, just sat in the chair looking at me. 'Well, I'm afraid you're totally wrong and I'm not listening to anything else you say.'

'That's your privilege.'

'Don't say it like that,' she cried.

'Like what?'

'All snooty. As though we're in court or something. Just talk to me like my friend.'

'I thought I was,' I murmured. Then I asked, 'So, what time are you due there?'

'You'd better whisper questions like that,' said Yolande. 'They've both got sharp hearing. I'm due there at half past nine tomorrow, and I should be home again by six o'clock at the latest.'

'Right, fine.' I didn't know what else to say after that.

'You really don't approve of any of this, do you?'

That took me by surprise. 'I never said that.'

'You don't have to. I can tell.' She went on, 'You want people to always be heroic and exciting and perfect. You want to put them up on pedestals, and if ever they do just one thing that disappoints you, you turn your back on them.'

I was hotly indignant now. 'Who have I turned my back on, then?' Then, answering my own question, 'And I hope you don't mean my grandad. If anything, he's turned his back on me.'

'I'm being mean to you, aren't I?' she said.

'Very mean.'

'Sorry – but it's just the way you keep looking at me.'

I smiled wanly. 'I shan't look at you again tonight.'

'You do expect a lot from people, you know.'

'Do I?'

'Oh yes,' she replied fervently. 'And no one wants to disappoint you, but sometimes they just can't help it.'

As I was leaving, I was about to whisper 'Good luck' to Yolande, but she said firmly, 'No, don't say anything about tomorrow, please.'

Later, though, I thought again about the things she'd said tonight. Especially about me not approving of what she was doing. It really wasn't like that. I just thought it wasn't something she should go through alone.

That's when I decided I'd surprise her and be there too. I'd stay the whole day. And then I'd take her home. I had enough money to pay for a taxi as well. She shouldn't be being jostled on a bus after what she'd just been through. So I'd look after her. I planned it all out in my head.

To explain my absence at home, I told Mum I was going to Cambridge with Yolande and her parents. I'd been chatting about Cambridge all evening to Yolande's parents (they'd even given me a list of places to visit), so I half felt as if I were going there anyway.

Mum seemed pleased for me. 'It'll do you good,' she said, and she gave me ten pounds extra spending money.

The following morning I left the house before Mum was awake. The clinic was at Stales, the nearest town to us. It was only about three miles away, and I walked there. It was a bright, crisp morning and I reached Stales quite quickly. It took me ages to find the clinic, though. I had to ask this woman, and she gave me such an odd look. But she directed me there. It was tucked away behind the hospital.

I arrived before the place had even opened up. I paced about and then, just after nine o'clock, Yolande arrived. I watched her walking towards the clinic. She looked as if she'd been awake for about twenty years. And my heart just flew out to her. I'd do everything I could to make this day a bit more bearable for her.

I sprang out. 'Hello, Yolande,' I cried, expecting a cry of total surprise. In fact, I'd been looking forward to that – but not for her to practically scream, 'What on earth are you doing here?'

I'd planned to say something rather dashing here like, 'I'm here for you, Yolande.' But her reaction threw me completely and I ended up muttering, 'Just thought I'd come along,' which I know sounded totally awful.

And she cried, 'This isn't a spectator sport, you know, Charlie.'

I just looked at her.

'Oh, Charlie,' she cried. 'If I'd wanted you to come along, don't you think I'd have asked you.' Her face was all red and sweaty. And then she started to cry, great tearing sobs that made her whole body shake.

I gaped at her in absolute horror.

I moved forward to try and comfort her or do something. But she just gulped, 'No, don't, please . . . please.' She screeched that last 'please' at me.

So I stepped back from her. I stood there, hanging my head, as if I'd just been told off by the headmaster or something. I felt so awkward and totally, totally useless.

'Charlie, will you just go home.' She sounded annoyed, yet there was a note of pleading in her voice too.

'If that's what you want,' I muttered.

'It really is,' she said, wiping her eyes with a tissue. 'I'd rather you didn't even watch me walk in, if you don't mind.'

'No, I don't mind. Will you ring me after . . . ring me later?'

She didn't answer, just gave me this quick glance. And she looked so scared, I really wanted to go after her. But I couldn't. So in the end I just sloped off. I'd expected Yolande to be pleased that I'd turned up. How could I have misjudged the situation so badly?

I should have realized she would rather be on her own. What was it she'd said to me? 'This isn't a spectator sport.' That really hurt.

I went and sat in Burger King for a while. But I wasn't

hungry at all. I just had about four sips of coffee.

Then I left a message on Yolande's mobile. I said, 'Sorry for barging in this morning. Give me a ring when you can. Thinking about you.' I guessed she wouldn't call me until this evening.

But, in fact, she rang just after eleven o'clock.

'Yolande,' I cried. 'How are you? What's happening?'

'What's happening is I couldn't go through with it, so I walked out . . .'

'Was that because of me?'

'Not really. Well, partly . . . I don't know.' She sounded very weary.

'Don't worry, it doesn't matter,' I said quickly. 'Look, do you want to meet up?'

'Not right now. I just want to be on my own for a bit.'

'Ring me later, then. Ring me any time.'

'Goodbye, Charlie.'

I wondered if she was wandering about the town like me. I guessed that she was. I hoped I could 'accidentally' bump into her. I went round every part of the town, but I never found her. Then I wandered into a cafe. I thought I must be hungry by now, so I ordered some food. Only I couldn't even bear to look at it. I pushed it away and sat staring into space, thinking about Yolande and my grandad . . . even my dad. The bad thoughts just kept rolling in.

And time was stuck. That morning was just endless. But I didn't really want to go home, so in the end I decided to visit the library. I saw this haggard old guy shuffling out of there with a pile of books under his arm. For a few moments I didn't even recognize Grandad. Can you believe that?

And it wasn't just the way this old man was stumbling along in a very un-Grandad-like way. It was that he looked so crushed, as if he were weighed down by some great worry.

He saw me and immediately straightened up. 'Ah, hello there,' he said, seeming to come back from somewhere faraway.

'Hi, Grandad,' I cried, and I wanted to say something else. In fact there were so many things I wanted to say. But all the words just shrivelled and died in my throat. I'd never felt so awkward and ill at ease with him.

'Been stocking up on my thrillers,' said Grandad, patting the books.

'So I see.' Then there was what seemed like a massive silence, though it probably only lasted a few seconds. It's just that usually Grandad and I chatted away so easily. We had our silences, of course, but they were easy, companionable ones. This one felt quite different.

I cried out, 'Do you fancy going off and having a cup of coffee or something?'

'Another time maybe,' said Grandad. 'But I'm rather pushed right now. In fact, I was supposed to be home half an hour ago.'

'Oh, right.' My voice fell away. 'See you later, then.'

Grandad nodded, then added, 'Stay safe, Charlie.' He often said that to me when I was leaving. It was like proof that the old grandad was still in there somewhere.

He tried to walk away in his usual, jaunty way. But I

knew he was just doing it for my benefit. That wasn't how he really felt. It was just more pretending, actually. He was dying inside. And so was I. Then I wondered for the seven-hundredth time just how we'd ended up like this.

I know what your answer would be. You'd blame me. You'd say Grandad had parcelled up all his memories of the Blackshirts a long time ago and left them in the darkest, most faraway part of his memory – until I came blundering along and disturbed them.

And, you know what, you're completely right. It was all my fault. I would just point out one fact to you: I didn't mean to find out about Grandad being in the Blackshirts. I didn't go searching for that information or anything.

But now that I'd discovered it, it was hanging in the air between Grandad and me all the time – and sucking the life out of both of us. Was there a way out of this? There had to be, otherwise we were both stuck in this no man's land. And I couldn't bear that.

I sat in the library, not reading anything, just thinking. I decided I might concentrate better if I put my head down in my hands. I'd just assumed this position when a woman tapped me on the shoulder and asked me if I were feeling ill. She wasn't even a librarian.

I assured her that I was in perfect health, but I don't think she believed me. She kept watching me anxiously, as if expecting me to keel over on to the floor at any moment. So I grabbed a newspaper and flung it up in front of my face. The headlines swam about. There was one about proof being needed for something or other. And that sent an idea rippling through my head; the newspaper

I was holding actually started to shiver. All at once I knew what I had to do.

I had to confront Grandad with the photograph. Let him see the proof.

I knew it would be a very hard thing for him. That's why I would put it inside a letter. He could examine it in private, without anyone watching him.

I started to compose the letter in my head. It would say something like:

Dear Grandad

I've hated these last few days and I think you have too. I know I've upset you and I'm truly sorry about that.

I did go and see Mr Perkins, SORRY. He told me you and he were in the Blackshirts together. He also showed me a photograph.

Will you please talk to me about this? Just a few words will be enough. And I swear on my life I will never raise this matter with you again.

With my kindest regards and all my love,
Charlie

PS I enclose the very photograph that Mr Perkins showed me.

Seeing this picture might jolt Grandad into telling me the truth. I know that would be pretty ghastly, but it was absolutely necessary. It was as if I were giving him medicine: bitter and nasty in the short term, but overall it'd make him – and me – feel so much better.

And it really was the only way we could break the spell that Mr Perkins had cast over us. But I wouldn't press Grandad on any point. I'd believe everything he told me. Then the crisis would be over. And the case closed forever.

There was just one huge snag to my plan: how on earth could I persuade Mr Perkins to let me borrow his precious photo? I bet he wouldn't even talk to me after the way I had disrupted his meeting. He'd just slam the door in my face. Well, I'd have to keep ringing on the doorbell until he did open up and at least give me a chance to explain.

And I would tell him I needed the photograph for Grandad to see. I'd also explain that I was only borrowing it and I would post it back to him. Would he believe me, though? I'd probably have to leave something behind as a sign of good faith, like my watch for instance. That was a present from Grandad, and a pretty expensive one too. But it should swing the deal all right.

I bombed out of the library. It was half past three. The sky was dark and heavy and an air of despair seemed to envelop everyone, except me. All at once I was in surprisingly good spirits because I was actually doing something. I was on a mission: I was going to get the photograph, deliver the letter – and, who knows, maybe Grandad and I could have everything sorted out between us by the end of tonight. Wouldn't that be brilliant?

At a quarter to four I jumped on the bus to Mr Perkins's house. I would be there in half an hour. One last visit – and then I'd be rid of him forever.

Chapter Twenty-two

Something happened at Mr Perkins's house that I hadn't anticipated: he wasn't in.

I don't know why, but I'd never imagined him going out. I assumed he always haunted that house. But the doorbell played 'Rule Britannia' seven times and there was no reply. Then I hammered on the door. Still nothing.

I decided he hadn't gone far, though – probably just down the road to stock up on his 'vice'. So I waited for him.

Half an hour limped past, still no sign and now the rain was pattering down.

Of course, Mr Perkins could be asleep somewhere. Or maybe he was just hiding from me. So many thoughts were racing through my head. And when you've got yourself really worked up to do something, there's all this energy jumping about inside you . . . and you can't just stay still, can you?

132

So in the end I went and opened Mr Perkins's side gate. It was highly unlikely that Mr Perkins was sitting in his back garden, but all this waiting about was unbearable. I took a quick look around. Like Grandad's, this garden was clearly tended lovingly. But it was much more regimented and ordered, with rows of plants lined up opposite each other like opposing teams.

I peeped inside the conservatory: very small, with just space for a wicker chair and a little table with heaps of newspapers on. No sign of Mr Perkins. I tried the conservatory door, never really expecting . . . It opened right away.

I was amazed. I'd assumed Mr Perkins's house would be like a fortress: locks and bolts all over the place. Actually, there was a padlock on the conservatory door with the key still in it. Did that mean Mr Perkins was lurking about somewhere?

Next I tried the door that led into the kitchen. It opened at once . . . It was almost as if Mr Perkins were inviting me into his home. Or was this just a trap?

I stepped forward very warily, as if there were unexploded bombs under the floorboards and I was trying very hard not to disturb them. I still wondered if Mr Perkins was suddenly going to lurch out at me.

I advanced into the hall; still no sign of him. This was so weird. If Mr Perkins was away, then what was to stop me nipping into his study right now and swiping that picture out of the album? Absolutely nothing. Especially as I remembered exactly where he kept the album – in the second drawer of his desk.

Of course, technically speaking I was stealing. Only I wasn't really as I was taking a picture of a relative (That's no excuse!) and I fully intended to bring – or at least post – it back. So I was only borrowing it for twenty-four hours.

That's what I told myself anyhow. But, to be honest, nothing could have stopped me seizing that photo. I'd convinced myself it was the key to everything. Armed with it, I could reconcile Grandad and me. So I just refused to listen to any moral scruples I might normally have had and was up those creaking stairs in a flash.

I opened the study door extremely carefully, though. If Mr Perkins were hiding anywhere, this is where it would be. But the room was empty.

It was as gloomy and musty as I remembered it, though. I never, ever thought I'd be returning here. Yet somehow he had dragged me back into its depths once more.

I sat down on the swivel chair. The ashtray was over-flowing. Mr Perkins had certainly been indulging his vice lately. There was a coffee cup here too, and his glasses. I pictured him sitting in this dark, grisly room, smoking away and thinking his twisted thoughts. Then, realizing I didn't have a moment to lose, I opened the second drawer and pulled out the album. I was sure this was it. I flicked hurriedly through its pages. There were lots of family snaps, mainly of weddings, all very formal.

Then, right in the middle of them I came across a picture of Mr Perkins in his Blackshirts uniform looking so intense and eager, it made me draw back in horror. I bet he was a truly vile teenager.

I turned over the page. There it was, waiting for me.

Only it seemed to have faded since I'd last seen it. Gone a little blurry. Or maybe it just seemed sharper and clearer in my head. Anyway, it still made my flesh crawl.

I snatched the photo up and shoved it into my pocket. I had it. Mission accomplished. But I didn't feel at all triumphant. Instead, a great shudder ran through me. It was this room: the smoky darkness crept inside you, getting right into your bones and blood.

I couldn't wait to leave. I sprang up from the swivel chair. Then I heard Mr Perkins talking very quietly downstairs. That gave me such a jolt I rocked back, sending the ashtray crashing. It exploded into bits, glittering all over the floor. Cigarette stubs were scattered everywhere too.

I stood there, paralysed with horror. Now what was I to do? Mr Perkins was certain to have heard that, wasn't he? I strained to make out what was going on downstairs. He'd stopped talking. Before, he'd sounded as if he were on the phone . . . his voice surprisingly low and grave.

Then I could detect him moving about. It seemed as if he hadn't heard me after all. He was just carrying on as usual. That was a break. I still had to get out of here unseen, though.

And then I heard Mr Perkins thumping up the stairs. I froze. Did he know I was up here? Or was he just off to his bedroom? He seemed to be getting up those stairs remarkably quickly, as if he were in a big hurry.

'I know you're up here,' he cried out suddenly.

I sucked in a huge, terrified breath.

'So come on, declare yourself.'

There was this awful, swelling quiet like a balloon about to burst.

I didn't know what to do.

'I should warn you, I am armed,' he announced.

And then the study door started opening.

Chapter Twenty-three

Mr Perkins was standing right in front of me. And he was indeed armed. He was holding his stick in one hand – and a sword in the other.

Goodness knows where he'd got it from, it looked about two hundred years old. And he was so worked up, I don't think he even saw me at first. He was too busy waving that sword about.

'Hello, Mr Perkins.' I struggled to make my voice sound as natural as possible, as if him finding me in his study on a Saturday afternoon wasn't anything out of the ordinary.

He let out a sharp cry of surprise. And then his shoulders sagged and the sword drooped in his arms. 'Oh no, this is too much,' he whispered, his voice filled with exhaustion.

'I'm very sorry for startling you,' I began.

Mr Perkins looked straight through me. He seemed

disorientated, as if he couldn't quite focus on what was happening now.

'Are you in on this?' he demanded suddenly.

'In on what?'

He sighed heavily. 'You knew I'd be out, didn't you?'

'No.'

He stared at me. 'So you don't know where I've just been?'

'No . . . Where have you just been?'

'To the hospital.'

That gave me a start. 'What were you . . . I mean, have you been ill?'

He didn't answer, just went on staring at me, suspicion radiating from him like heat. 'You didn't know about the attack on my son, then?'

'No I didn't,' I cried at once. 'What happened?'

'He was innocently canvassing this afternoon when he was set upon by thugs. A rock was thrown at him.' He gave a long, trembling gasp. 'He had to be rushed to hospital. I was all set to meet him at five o'clock for his big rally. Instead, I receive a phone call saying he's been rushed to hospital. Have you any idea how worried I've been? I'm over eighty, you know.' He pointed a finger accusingly at me, as if I were somehow involved in that attack too.

The rally. I had completely forgotten about that. Yolande and I were supposed to be going along. Suddenly I remembered Raymond saying how he was going to try to sabotage Gerald Perkins's meetings. Well, he might have thrown another water bomb – but not stones. This couldn't have anything to do with him.

'How is your son?' I asked.

'They don't know yet. They've got to keep him in for observation.' He started wagging a finger at me again. 'What's happened to free speech in this country? Why has everything got to be politically correct?' His voice went all whiny.

But this wasn't the moment for a discussion, so I didn't reply. I even felt the faint stirrings of sympathy for him, which I promptly squashed. I couldn't waste time feeling sorry for him.

Then he came out of his rant and looked at me as if he'd just seen me for the first time. 'What are you doing in my house . . .? My ashtray!' he cried suddenly, noticing all the bits of glass sprinkled across the floor.

'I'm so sorry about that,' I said, speaking very quietly. 'I'll pay for it, of course. Just let me know what it cost. And as for being in your house, well, I just dropped by to borrow a photograph. Only you weren't in, so I very cheekily helped myself.'

'What photograph?' he asked, though I think he knew.

'It's the one you showed me of you and Grandad at the Blackshirts rally.'

'And why on earth do you wish to borrow that?' He sounded tired and bewildered.

'I thought Grandad ought to see it.'

'Why?' He snapped the question out in an uncharacteristically sharp way.

'Well, I just thought that he needed to see it,' I concluded lamely.

'But you had no business breaking in . . .'

'I didn't exactly break in. The back door was open . . .'

'You broke in,' cried Mr Perkins, 'and stole something of mine that you will return to me now.'

'Would you mind very much if I just borrowed it for twenty-four hours?'

'Yes, I would. I'm appalled by the breakdown of law and order in this country,' he cried, his face twisted with disgust. 'People attacked in the street for holding an opinion, break-ins, burglaries everywhere.' He tottered forward, his forehead slicked with sweat. 'Give me back my property, then I shall call the police.'

'Oh no, please don't do that,' I said desperately.

Mr Perkins saw my sudden discomfort and pounced on it. 'But what are you afraid of? You want something, so you've got to have it, it's as simple as that in your modern, multicultural society, isn't it?'

'Look, I'll pay for borrowing the photograph – and as for the ashtray, how much do you want? Name your price,' I cried.

But Mr Perkins didn't seem to have heard me as he hissed, 'Do you know what? I hope the police throw the book at you: breaking in, stealing, vandalism. You might even end up in prison.'

'For borrowing one little photograph?' Anger was tingling in every part of my body now. 'And anyway, you caused all this. Grandad and I were very happy until you barged your way into our lives with all your nasty stories and then that photograph, which you just had to show me, didn't you?' My voice tight with fury now, I went on, 'You provoked me into this. And you've brought it all on yourself because you're a bitter, frustrated man –'

'Enough,' cried Mr Perkins. 'Return my property and then leave my home.' And as he said this he raised the sword again. Normally I would have just laughed. I mean, what was he going to do with that antique? But right then I was so angry and frustrated with him that I waved my right hand in a move of general exasperation. And I suppose I did wave it in his direction.

I'd never, ever have hit Mr Perkins, though. I wish to make that very clear. First of all, because of his age. Also, I'm not a violent person at all, plus I'm useless at fighting anyhow. Yet Mr Perkins obviously didn't know any of that, because he staggered back from me in alarm and temporarily lost his balance; his arms flailed about, while his stick and sword went clanging to the floor. Then he fell back on to a chair – he wasn't hurt or anything – but he landed abruptly and started breathing very rapidly.

And I should have stayed to help him and seen if he was all right. Instead, all I did was pick up his stick and fling it down beside him. After which I scarpered off like a burglar who'd just been disturbed.

I was so worked up, I ran all the way to the bus stop, and when I was on the bus I couldn't stop shivering, while my heart was still going *thump*, *thump*, *thump*, like a continual drumbeat.

Would Mr Perkins really call the police? Maybe after he'd calmed down he'd realize I hadn't actually done him any harm. It was those people who'd attacked his son he was really angry with. I just happened to catch him at the wrong moment.

I wished I'd checked that he was OK before I left, though. What if he had some sort of seizure? No, he'd be all right. He was sitting down when I left him. But what a total and complete mess. Still, at least I had the photograph. And, if relations between Grandad and me got back to normal as a result of that, it would have been more than worth it.

Then I noticed there was a message waiting for me on my mobile.

Yolande.

That was my first and only thought. It had to be her. In fact, it was Raymond.

'Just to let you know, Charlie, if you and Yolande were thinking about coming to the rally at five o'clock – well, it's been cancelled. Perkins was out canvassing earlier and the Fighters Against Fascism were there protesting. But then someone else came along and threw a brick at him. Cut his face open. And he's in hospital now.

'The Fighters Against Fascism regret such violence. But people like Perkins clearly incite such behaviour with their racist views.

'Give me a ring if you require a fuller update.'

I thought about what Raymond said, but only for a moment. My head was too full of the blinding disappointment that it hadn't been Yolande calling me. I was so agitated, I even switched off my mobile by mistake.

I wondered where Yolande was now. Was she back at home, telling her parents about the lovely day in Cambridge she'd spent with me?

I hoped she was all right.

I was very tempted to ring her. But I didn't want her to feel I was crowding her or anything.

Later, walking home, I wondered if Mum would be full of questions about my imaginary visit to Cambridge. I'd have to say Yolande and I went on the river . . .

And then everything else just flew out of my head. For right outside my house was a police car.

I had this sense of a dream-like unreality closing in on me. I walked forward very slowly, my knees as weak as water. Then Mum saw me and dashed out of the house. She was practically bursting with relief. 'Oh, there you are. Thank goodness.' But she looked very confused as well. She whispered to me as if she were passing on a secret message, 'The police have just come round with some ridiculous story that you'd broken into an old man's house. I said that was total nonsense. You were in Cambridge with your girlfriend and her family. So when I couldn't get an answer from your mobile, I rang Yolande's house to see if you were back yet . . .'

The breath caught in my throat. 'You rang Yolande's house?' I quavered.

'Yes, I spoke to her mother, who seemed to think you were with me in Cambridge. What's going on, Charlie?' She looked at me, puzzled but still hopeful that I could clear all this up.

And then I saw the policemen waiting for me in the doorway.

Chapter Twenty-four

There were two of them. One was very young – didn't look much older than me, in fact – and very restless. While I was talking, he looked at me with a mixture of disbelief and impatience as if he couldn't wait for me to stop babbling since it was all rubbish anyway.

The other was much older: burly, like a PE teacher who still kept himself very fit. He was calmer and spoke very quietly. Still, when he asked you a question, his eyes stayed on your face, really drilling into you. You felt he didn't miss a thing.

Explaining to them what had happened was ghastly, especially with Mum sitting in on the interview as well.

'So you broke into Mr Perkins's home just to take away a photograph?' said the younger policeman, his voice positively buzzing with incredulity.

'Sure you didn't take anything else?' The older man whispered this.

'No, nothing.'

'Do you have any idea,' asked the younger policeman, 'how frightening it is to find someone wandering around your house?'

'No – I mean, yes, I can imagine how frightening that would be,' I said.

'And Mr Perkins is a pensioner,' the younger one persisted. 'He is kind to you and helps you to research your grandfather's past.' He waited for me to agree with him, but I couldn't. Mr Perkins had never been kind to me. He'd set out to make trouble from the very start. That didn't excuse what I had done. But there was no point in pretending he was an innocent victim in all this.

The younger policeman noticed my silence and gave a snort of disdain. 'So where is this photograph now?'

'I'm not exactly sure.' I didn't want them looking at that picture of Grandad as a Blackshirt. That was nothing to do with them.

'You break into a house to steal a photograph, and now you say you've lost it?' The younger policeman was incredulous.

'I haven't exactly lost it –' I began.

The older policeman cut in. 'Well, you will need to bring it with you to the police station, where you'll have to make a full statement at eleven o'clock tomorrow. Is that clear?'

'Yes,' I replied.

Then he looked at Mum.

'He will be there,' said Mum, who'd been listening intently to all this.

They both got up then and they stayed talking to Mum for a few more minutes in the hallway. When Mum returned, she was looking exceedingly grim. I was standing by the window with my head bowed. 'What were you thinking of, forcing your way into that old man's house?' she demanded.

'I didn't force my way inside, Mum, I just wandered in.'

'Well, that's not how the police see it. You'd no business in that old man's house. I'm very surprised at you. I'd never have thought you'd do something as stupid as that. I'm seeing you in a new light tonight.'

I was seeing myself in a new light too. In fact, right now I wasn't quite sure who I was any more.

'Well, sit down so that I can talk to you properly,' she said. 'You could be in very serious trouble.'

'I know.'

We both sat down, while the rain started up again, splashing and beating against the window. Mum usually just lets me go my own way. I know she trusts me completely. So she and I had never had a really big showdown before.

She began, 'Your grandad asked you not to see this Mr Perkins, didn't he?'

'Yes, he did,' I admitted.

'So why did you?'

'I'd seen him already. And I wanted to clear Grandad's name.'

Mum's eyebrows shot up. 'What do you mean?'

'Well, he was saying some things about Grandad.'

'What sort of things?'

I stared miserably at my hands. I hated repeating any of this to Mum. 'Well, he said how Grandad was really badly behaved and was always in trouble and he got expelled from school . . .' I stopped. I couldn't bring myself to go on about the Blackshirts.

Mum looked at me. 'Well, actually, he *was* expelled from school.'

'Oh, I never knew that.'

'And did you need to?' she demanded.

'No,' I began.

'Your grandad had a horrible childhood, especially losing his mother so young. The whole centre of his world was just knocked away after that. He was never close to his father either. I don't know all the reasons. But his father went from job to job, and he had a drink problem. I can't tell you any more because your grandad never liked talking about those days and –' she gave me a sharp look – 'I respected that.' She went on, 'I see you've taken down all your grandfather's pictures from your bedroom. Was that because he was expelled from school and –'

'No, no,' I protested. That sounded totally pathetic. 'It's more complicated than that.'

Mum gave me one of her piercing stares. 'You suspect Grandad of not being perfect, so you banish him from your walls . . .'

I shook my head vigorously. 'That's not it at all.'

'And are you perfect?' she persisted.

'I really am not,' I said.

'But you're allowed to be less than perfect?'

I didn't answer that.

Mum was silent for a moment. I could almost hear her thinking. 'Now, this photograph you took. Why exactly did you want that?'

'I just thought it was something Grandad should see,' I said vaguely, fervently wishing this interrogation would stop. This was actually worse than being interviewed by the police.

'Can I see it?' she asked.

'If you want to,' I said, hoping I didn't sound as reluctant as I felt.

'Well, I don't want to,' said Mum, 'because that ancient photograph has got absolutely nothing to do with your grandad and me. It's got nothing to do with you and Grandad either.'

I couldn't agree with her on that one, but I didn't dare argue with Mum. Not in her present mood.

'You know, *you* see more of your grandad now,' she went on, 'than *I* ever did when I was growing up.'

That really surprised me. 'But how come?' I asked.

'Well, you know he was a civilian pilot after the war. Then, after he retired from flying, he became a travelling representative for the company, so he was never able to be at home for very long. I was sad about that, but I learnt to take him as I found him. And when he was there he was great. I'll tell you something else.' Her voice rose. 'Whenever I turned to him for help, he came up trumps every single time.'

I could imagine that: Grandad as some mysterious figure never around for long – yet always riding to the rescue when he was needed. Well, look how he'd helped Mum and me after Dad died.

Mum leant forward. 'Right, get me Mr Perkins's phone number.'

I gaped at her. 'What do you want that for?'

'To try and get you out of this mess.'

I was still staring at her. 'Why?'

She suddenly smiled at me – it was like the sun coming out. 'Because that's what mothers do, Charlie, even when you've been totally irresponsible. So come on, let me see if I can sort this out for you.'

A few minutes later, she called up Mr Perkins, but there was no reply. And then our phone rang. It was Nan. A neighbour had spotted a police car outside our house and had very kindly informed Nan of this fact. Mum briefly told her what had happened. Nan was very shocked. Grandad was out, taking Gertie for a walk at the time. And Mum said to me afterwards, 'I've suggested that Nan doesn't tell Grandad you saw Mr Perkins today, as it might upset him.'

Shortly afterwards, Mum left for the last night of her play. She took some persuading, but I assured her I had done my share of housebreaking for the day and didn't need watching.

She said she'd try to contact Mr Perkins again as well. But I wasn't holding my breath. I seriously doubted if Mum could talk him round. He was clearly out for vengeance.

Mum had been so distracted by Mr Perkins, she totally forgot to ask me why I'd pretended I'd visited Cambridge today. But I bet Yolande wasn't so lucky. After my mum's phone call, was Yolande's cover well and truly blown? I dreaded finding out, yet I really had to know as well. So, the moment Mum left, I called her.

'I've been trying to call you,' she said. 'What's this about the police wanting to speak to you?'

'Oh, that's not important,' I said quickly. 'What happened about my mum calling?'

'Well, that did give my parents a massive clue that I wasn't in Cambridge.' But Yolande said this quite lightly. 'Then I came in, warbling about what a wonderful day you and I had had in Cambridge . . .'

'Oh no,' I groaned.

'Oh yes . . . and then . . . well, sometimes, you know, it's just less hassle to tell them the truth.'

That took me by surprise. 'So they know?'

'Yes, they do.'

'And what happened? I mean, how did they react?'

'As I expected, really. Very shocked that their sweet, innocent daughter could ever become pregnant. I told them I'm still not completely sure what I'm going to do. And we're going to have a family meeting about it tomorrow. What fun! But they said the final decision is mine and, whatever I decide, they'll go every step of the way with me.'

'So that's all right.'

'Yes, yes,' agreed Yolande. 'I can't complain about them at all, except they keep asking me who the father is. And that really is none of their business.'

'Won't they guess it's Callum's, though?' I asked.

'They'd guess wrong, then.' She lowered her voice to

just above a whisper. 'I went totally off the rails with Callum. I was mad about him for a while.'

'I noticed.'

'Then he dumped me and I thought I'd lost this great chunk of my life.' Her voice rose mock-dramatically. 'And I just couldn't go on living without him. I even went and begged him to go out with me again.'

'Oh, Yolande,' I cried.

'I know. But anyway, he told me he couldn't.'

'Why not?'

'He said there was no spark between us any more. Well, that just made me feel completely worthless. And, let me tell you, that's when you're at your most dangerous. You can do anything, feeling like that. You can even get drunk out of your head at a party with a boy you can hardly remember and didn't even like much anyway . . .'

'And he's the father?'

'That's a secret between the two of us,' she hissed. 'All right?'

'All right,' I agreed.

'Oh, Charlie, I'm sixteen, for goodness' sake. But right now I feel as if I've just aged ten years overnight. I'm so old, suddenly.'

'We can sort it out,' I said.

'You make it sound like maths homework . . . but thank you. Now, come on, what did the police want to see you about?'

I told her briefly what had happened.

'Oh, how could you be so stupid . . . honestly, you need a keeper sometimes.'

'You'll come and visit me in prison, won't you?'

'Now you're just being silly,' said Yolande.

'No, that's Mr Perkins's ambition, to have me locked up.'

'Have you shown your grandad this photograph?'

'No, I haven't,' I replied. 'And I don't know if I will now.'

'What!'

'I was worked up, I was all over the place.'

'So all that hassle was for absolutely nothing.' Then she hissed, 'Look, my parents are circling. They are smothering me a bit tonight but I can't say anything, since they mean well. You'll be fine tomorrow, Charlie. I'm sure of it. Just look desperately sorry and roll those wonderful eyes of yours about. And try and get a good night's sleep, so you're fresh and alert tomorrow.'

Of course I had a terrible night's sleep. So, I'm sure, did Mum, as I could hear her downstairs before seven o'clock. She insisted on cooking us both breakfast. I think she just wanted something to do, since neither of us ate much of it.

She was rehearsing with me what I should say at the police station when the phone rang. Mum's voice was quite low and I couldn't hear what she was saying. Her tone sounded serious, though. I wondered if it was the police again. But it wasn't.

'That was your grandad,' she announced. 'He called to say that there is no need for you to go to the police station as he has spoken to Mr Perkins – who has dropped all the charges.'

I gaped at her. 'So Nan told Grandad –'

'Yes, she thought he'd want to know,' Mum interrupted me. 'He tried ringing Mr Perkins last night but couldn't get any answer. It was only this morning he finally reached him.'

'I wonder what Grandad said to him,' I murmured. It must have been so weird, those two talking again after more than half a century. I was totally stunned by this turn of events, actually.

'It can't have been an easy conversation for your grandad,' said Mum.

'No, it can't,' I agreed.

'Now he wants you to go round and see him,' went on Mum. 'And he specially asked if you would bring that photo with you.'

Chapter Twenty-five

Nan opened the door. I shuffled in, a bit awkwardly. I thought she might be angry with me for seeing Mr Perkins. Or start interrogating me about that photograph. But she just said, 'I'm slipping out for a while – so I'll leave you boys to it.'

Nan often said something like that. Only today I could hear the anxiety in her voice.

'He's waiting for you,' she continued, 'and I know you'll be understanding, Charlie.'

That made me feel really bad. I hadn't come here to judge Grandad. That wasn't it at all. 'I just want to clear a few things up,' I said.

Nan ruffled my hair. 'Of course, and it'll be fine . . . you and he share so much . . . it'll be fine,' she said again, but more to herself than to me. Then she added, 'He's in the dining room.'

The dining room was usually only used at night.

Normally at this time Grandad would be in the kitchen, relaxing over the paper, or taking Gertie for a walk. But today he was sitting behind the oval mahogany table, as if he were waiting to start a board meeting. I'd never seen him look so serious. He was wearing his favourite jacket, the one he usually saved for special occasions. Only today it hung loose from his shoulders. And I realized with a shock how much weight he'd lost recently.

I plastered a smile on my face. 'Hey, Grandad, thanks so much for talking to Mr Perkins for me.' I was trying to sound normal, but I could feel my face burning and burning.

'It was because of me you were there. So it was up to me to sort things out,' Grandad replied in the brisk tones he usually reserved for discussions on his health. 'Now sit down.' He motioned me to sit opposite him. 'Did you bring that photo?' he asked.

'I did.'

There was a pause.

'Do you want to see it now?' I asked.

'Yes, I think I do, Charlie,' he said quietly.

I dug into my pocket. My hands were trembling. I slid the photograph across the table. He picked it up and studied it as if it were a playing card he'd just been handed. I couldn't read his expression at all.

'Never thought I'd see this again.' He spoke like someone who'd just discovered a long-lost piece of luggage. Then he slammed it down.

I started to breathe again. I thought the photograph might really disturb him, but he seemed remarkably calm about it.

'I can see why you'd want me to see it,' he said slowly. Then he got up. 'I think it's time for a cup of tea now, don't you?'

He was on his feet and making for the door before I could reply. 'Do you want a hand?' I asked.

'No, no, it's all ready.'

He was gone for ages. I wondered if I should go after him, but perhaps he wanted a bit of time on his own. Maybe seeing that picture had been more traumatic than he was letting on.

He finally returned, clattering a tray of tea. 'Here we are,' he said. Then he exclaimed, 'Would you believe – I've forgotten the sugar.' He was off again before I could say I didn't really care about the sugar.

He returned, waving the sugar bowl as if he'd just won it. Then, after helping me to my tea, he didn't sit down. Instead, he stared out of the window.

'So have you got a list of questions for me to tackle, then?' he asked.

This was awful: Grandad was treating me as if I were a policeman interrogating a suspect. 'I just wondered why you –?'

'Why I was in the Blackshirts? That's what's bothering you so much, isn't it?' interrupted Grandad.

'I just wanted to understand . . .' I began desperately. 'Maybe you could tell me a little bit about it . . .'

For a few moments Grandad just went on gazing out of the window. 'Going to be a nice day,' he said at last.

'Yes,' I agreed. Pale sunlight was spilling through the

curtains, while out in the garden Grandad's cherry tree was already ablaze with blossom.

'The world's never so bad when you've got the sun on your back,' said Grandad suddenly. 'My mother said that. I was not an easy child, you know. I think I was born a tearaway, but my mother had a huge, kind heart . . . and when she died I had such a rage inside me. She was only thirty-four. No age at all. It was the injustice of it. A good woman like her, dying so young. I just couldn't accept it.' He turned round. 'I didn't care about anything after that. Certainly not school. I hated school and school hated me. While my dad . . . he did try – but life was too much for him, too hard. I could see him going under. He wasn't the only one. In those days, if you were poor you had absolutely nothing. You *were* nothing. I still think the country needed a bloody revolution then.'

He gave a dry little laugh. Then he walked back to the table, but he didn't sit down. Instead, he stood in front of me with his hands behind his back, just as if he were a defendant on trial.

'I was angry all the time, the anger that eats away at your insides, like a kind of sickness. Do you understand?'

'Yes, Grandad,' I said, 'I really do.' These last few days, I'd been consumed with a deep, burning fury against Mr Perkins. I could see how that might go on and on.

'Then along came the Blackshirts, offering brotherhood and a way out,' said Grandad. 'The government didn't care about ordinary people like me, but the Blackshirts did. They were going to eliminate poverty – and class.

They were going to bring in a new, fairer society. They had the answers to everything. They made me feel strong and looked after.' He took a breath. 'Of course, things soon got ugly. There were fights . . . beating up people.'

'Did you . . .?' I began. Then I stopped. Could I really ask Grandad that? But he finished the question for me.

'Did I join in any of that?' he said.

'You really don't need to answer that, Grandad,' I cried. 'It's not at all important.'

'Yes, it is,' he said in a thick, strained voice. 'Let's say I was on the fringes of it. I kidded myself that this was a necessary stage before we created this wonderful, fairer world. But I knew . . .' He lowered his head and in an awful, croaking whisper said, 'This is the hard part now, Charlie.'

I felt myself trembling. My palms began to sweat. 'Stop now, Grandad,' I cried desperately. 'You've told me enough. Really.'

But he went on in that same, expressionless tone, his head still lowered. 'I knew exactly how violent the Blackshirts had become, but I closed that part of my mind down. Just refused to listen to it. That's the truth, I'm afraid.' He looked up and his eyes met mine. 'After a bit, you'd think I'd have got all my anger at the world out of my system – used it all up. But the truth is, once you invite those feelings into your life, they're very hard to get rid of . . . Remember that, Charlie.' His eyes stayed on my face.

'I will,' I said quietly.

'In the end I did leave the Blackshirts. No big

denunciation, I'm afraid. I just drifted away from them, totally disillusioned –'

'And then you became a fighter pilot,' I interrupted, 'and found your true self.'

Grandad snorted. 'Want to know the truth about that? I never thought I'd survive the war. I always thought, any moment now I'll be killed – and bloody good riddance. I didn't care if I came back or not. I mean, what did I have to come back to? Of course, in the RAF I found the very things I'd been looking for in the Blackshirts: comradeship and some kind of purpose to my life. But I wasn't especially brave.'

'What rubbish,' I began.

He raised a hand. 'Courage is being able to admit to your grandson you were a Blackshirt. But I funked that one. Told myself I was doing it for your benefit. You'd had enough trauma, losing your father so young. So I was keeping you safe from any more. Told myself you needed me to be a complete hero, when really I just didn't want you to know . . .'

'And that was your right –' I said.

'No, it wasn't,' interrupted Grandad. 'If you set yourself up as some kind of hero, take all the bows and glory, well, your life doesn't belong only to you any more. That's the deal.'

Suddenly he sank down in his chair. He picked up the photograph again and just stared into it for the longest time.

Then he murmured, 'Do you ever wish you could reach back through time and tell yourself . . . tell yourself . . .'

His shoulders began to shake. Tears were sliding down his face.

I'd never seen Grandad cry before. It was awful. I got to my feet. But he gave his neck a stiff-like shake. 'I'm all right, Charlie . . . It's just that sometimes the past can be very heavy.'

Then he let the photograph slip down and he gripped the edges of the table as if trying to steady himself.

In a low, flat voice he said, 'The moment you asked me about the Blackshirts, I knew the game was up . . . it was all over. And I decided you'd be much better off without me. I was just messing things up for you . . .'

'Messing things up?' I repeated disbelievingly. 'You've transformed my entire life.' My words seemed to echo round the room; I'd really bawled them out. 'And I couldn't have got through these past three years without you.'

'Hearing that makes me very happy,' said Grandad softly. 'Thank you.' Then he leant back in his chair. He looked utterly exhausted. 'Is there anything else you want to know?' he asked.

'Not a single thing,' I said firmly. It had seemed so important before. I just had to know the truth about Grandad and the Blackshirts. So Grandad had gone back into the darkness of those days – for me.

But now I was wondering, was it really so vital? Couldn't I have lived without knowing all that? Well, of course I could. What Grandad and I shared was deeper and stronger than anything Mr Perkins could throw at us. That was the real truth. Why couldn't I have seen that before?

'Well, I shall return this photograph to Maurice Perkins,' Grandad announced suddenly.

'What was it like, talking to him again after all those years?' I asked.

Grandad considered. 'Very strange . . . especially as I hadn't ever liked him very much.'

'He told me you were good mates.'

Grandad smiled faintly. 'Funny what we choose to remember.'

'So what was he like?' I asked.

'Well, I remember a boy who was always trying to latch on to people. He'd buy you sweets, which you'd take, then you'd tell him to clear off or make fun of him for wearing a chest protector . . . After I left, he wrote me two letters and I didn't reply to either of them.'

I laughed.

Grandad started to join in, but then he said, 'No, we shouldn't laugh at the poor devil. Actually, I think you might even owe him an apology.'

'Do you really?' I was surprised.

'Yes, I believe he deserves that.'

I didn't make much answer. But I didn't see how I could ever apologize to Perkins – not after all the misery he'd caused.

'Now don't be offended,' said Grandad, 'but would you mind popping off for a bit now, Charlie? So many memories have come back that I feel a bit giddy, as if I'd drunk a couple of glasses of wine. Just need a bit of time to . . .'

'Of course. I'd like to come back later, though.'

He looked surprised and pleased. 'And can you see

yourself out? I'm just going to sit here in this wonderful sun for a while.' It was really streaming through the window now.

'See you soon, then,' I said.

He smiled. 'Stay safe, Charlie.'

And I left him there, still half in the past.

Chapter Twenty-six

I did finally apologize to Mr Perkins.

Seven weeks later.

I knew Grandad wanted me to go – but I kept putting it off until that morning. And I didn't even ring Mr Perkins to see if he was in; I just turned up there. I was in a right state, actually.

Plastered across Mr Perkins's windows were the election posters for his son. The day after Gerald Perkins was struck by a brick, he was out of hospital and electioneering, with a bandage streaked right across his forehead. He made the front page of all the local papers. And I worried it might turn him into something of a hero.

Well, despite that bandage, he didn't win. Still, he didn't lose his deposit either. In fact, he came a very respectable third – which, as Raymond pointed out, shows you can't be too vigilant against people like Gerald Perkins.

I hovered on the doorstep. Could I really go through with this, apologize to someone as loathsome as Mr Perkins? But Grandad had asked me to do this. It was the only reason I was here, really.

I rang the doorbell. The strains of 'Rule Britannia' rang out once more. He was ages coming to the door. In fact, I was just on the point of going off again when he finally appeared. He gazed at me suspiciously, but curiosity gleamed out of his eyes too.

'Hello, Mr Perkins,' I said.

'Hello,' he replied warily. I wanted to run off then without apologizing, but that would have been just so childish. I had to go through with it now.

'I just came round to – very belatedly – say I'm extremely sorry for entering your house without permission. Also, for removing the photograph. And for accidentally smashing your ashtray. Please accept my total apology.'

Mr Perkins just went on staring at me as if I were a street performer or something. Face totally expressionless. 'Thank you,' he said stiffly.

'Grandad posted the photograph back to you, didn't he?'

'He did indeed,' said Mr Perkins. Some warmth came into his voice. 'He also wrote me a very gracious letter.' Then he added, 'I'm sorry I can't ask you in this time.'

'That's all right,' I said. Last thing I wanted to do was to spend any more time with that freak.

'You see, I've just returned from staying with my daughter and my grandchildren.' A note of pride entered his voice when he mentioned them. 'But I do accept your apology.'

I was about to turn away, my duty done, when he called, 'Please do thank your grandfather for his correspondence with me, and give him my best wishes.' I stared at him, stupefied. He saw the look on my face and asked, 'Is anything wrong?' But for a moment there I was so choked up I couldn't speak.

'But haven't you heard?' I said at last, my breath coming in jagged gasps. 'My grandad . . . he died two weeks ago.'

Mr Perkins leant forward heavily on his stick, shock twitching in his eyes. Then he went completely still. 'This is terrible news,' he said slowly. 'I had no idea.'

I was sure he'd have read about Grandad in the local papers. They did him proud with their obituaries. One headline said how Grandad had taken off on his final flight . . . I think he would have especially liked that one.

'I knew your grandfather was ill, but I thought he was . . .' His voice fell away.

'The doctors said he was a real fighter. But one morning he collapsed at home and had to be rushed into hospital –' I struggled to keep the tears from my voice – 'he died there the following day.'

'I'm so very sorry,' cried Mr Perkins. And he looked genuinely distressed – which was pretty odd when you think about it. After all, he'd only spoken to Grandad once in the past fifty years.

'Look, please come inside, Charlie.'

Don't ask me why, but I didn't resist. I allowed him to draw me inside his crypt once more.

My head was all over the place. And as I sat down in that weird dining room, I felt as if I were half there and half somewhere else. I'd only come because of a promise I'd made to Grandad, which I'd never kept. Then, this morning, I'd just woken up and thought: I'm going to do this for Grandad right now.

Mr Perkins insisted on making me a cup of tea, and as he handed me it he asked, 'Now, how's that for you?' as gently as if I were a little child or a scared puppy.

Mr Perkins kept going on about the letter Grandad had sent him. He seemed chuffed to bits with it, and so proud too, as if it had been penned by a famous person.

Then he said, 'At least there will be the statue of your grandfather to ensure he's never forgotten.' And I was so pleased I'd persuaded Grandad to relent on that one.

We talked for ages about Grandad, and all these little memories of him kept flashing through my head. Especially those last weeks . . . because that's when Grandad and I went over his story again. Only this time he said he didn't want it to be just about his war years but also what he called 'the jumble of all my other selves too'.

My mistake was wanting Grandad to have just one self called a 'hero'. In fact, every one of us has got so many selves. And different situations can bring these out. This means that no one can be labelled just a 'loser' or 'bad', or just a 'hero' either. There's more to everyone than that.

Do you know, I think I got to know Grandad better in those last weeks than ever before. He looked alarmingly thin and frail; but as soon as we started working, his eyes just shone with excitement. And he told such fascinating stories. His body might have got old, but he never did. I just wish it could have gone on longer.

The end was very sudden. One night I was round at his house interviewing him, as usual. The next I was sitting by his hospital bed. (Later, Nan told us how very ill Grandad had been during those last weeks. That was a secret he'd kept, even from Mum and me.) That night the nurse said he was slipping away from us. But I couldn't believe it. I sat there, whispering away to him, willing him back. And once his eyes actually fluttered open. He looked right at me and said my name, as if he were speaking out of a dream. And then he grasped my hand so tightly.

The next morning he was gone, and my whole world had gone with him.

'The days after the funeral are the hardest, aren't they?' said Mr Perkins to me suddenly.

I looked at him in total surprise. 'Yes, they are,' I said.

Immediately after Grandad had died there was this mad whirl of activity – so many people wanted to talk about him – and a mind-numbing sense of unreality too. I suppose that protects you really. It was only after the funeral that this feeling of total misery and emptiness ripped right through me. And afterwards I just seemed to carry around with me this horrible pain, like a lump of stone right in the middle of my stomach. I thought it had settled inside me forever.

But Mr Perkins continued, 'The pain you're feeling will get better . . . When I lost my Eileen, I thought I would never stop grieving for her, but little by little it does start getting better. You never get over your loss, but you can put it in a different place.'

Can't tell you how weird that was – being comforted and helped by, of all people, Mr Perkins.

Yes, a lot of his views might stink. And sometimes I imagined him bursting into my life in a puff of sulphur. But he wasn't really a demon. It's very easy to dehumanize people. Yet once you do that – once you stop seeing them as someone like you – that's when you're opening the door to cruelty and intolerance and fascism and all the evil words.

I left Mr Perkins's house surprisingly pleased that I'd visited him. I'd actually found some of the things he'd said quite helpful. And that was a massive surprise.

When I got outside, who was waiting for me but Yolande? I'd just left her a quick message on her mobile saying where I was going.

'What are you doing here?' I asked.

She shrugged and smiled.

'Come to see if I've nicked any more photographs, have you? Well, I'm clean, Miss. You can check if you like.'

She grinned and gave me a bit of a hug right outside Mr Perkins's house.

We've become such good friends. Of course, I can't stop this little hope bubbling up inside me from time to time that maybe one day she and I will be . . . So I haven't given up on that dream.

But honestly, her friendship hasn't just been some kind of consolation prize. The truth is, I couldn't have got through these last two weeks without her.

No, she hasn't had the abortion. And it looks increasingly as if she will have the baby – and then perhaps have it adopted. She's not totally sure about the adoption part. But I know she's been discussing it a lot with her parents.

Last night she and I went round to see Nan – and Gertie. Nan said she'd been sorting through some of Grandad's things. He'd told her I was to have his wartime photo album. And inside it she'd discovered an envelope addressed to me.

I opened it up, and there was a little card on which was written:

To Charlie

Just remember, the bond between us can never be broken. I'll always be there with you.

Your loving wonky-eyed Grandad.

And Grandad is still with me, in my thoughts, in my heart. Then I've got all those interviews he gave me. I don't feel quite ready to play the tapes yet. But one day I will.

What a story I shall have to tell you then.

Puffin by Post

The Hero Game – Pete Johnson

If you have enjoyed this book and want to read more,
then check out these other great Puffin titles.
You can order any of the following books direct with Puffin by Post:

Ten Hours to Live • Pete Johnson • 0141314222	£4.99
'A brilliantly moving book' – *The Times*	

The Protectors • Pete Johnson • 0141314214	£4.99
'A tautly written thriller about the use of power' – *Books for Keeps*	

Faking It • Pete Johnson • 0141315423	£4.99
'A wickedly funny writer' – *Mail on Sunday*	

I'd Rather Be Famous • Pete Johnson • 0141315466	£4.99
'A witty look at TV fame' – *Guardian*	

The Cool Boffin • Pete Johnson • 0141315458	£4.99
'One of the funniest books I have ever read' – *The Times*	

Just contact:

Puffin Books , c/o Bookpost, PO Box 29,
Douglas, Isle of Man, IM99 1BQ
Credit cards accepted. For further details:
Telephone: 01624 677237
Fax: 01624 670923

You can email your orders to: bookshop@enterprise.net
Or order online at: www.bookpost.co.uk

Free delivery in the UK.
Overseas customers must add £2 per book.

Prices and availability are subject to change.

Visit puffin.co.uk to find out about the latest titles, read extracts and
exclusive author interviews, and enter exciting competitions.
You can also browse thousands of Puffin books online.